Enid Blyton's
TEN MINUTE
TALES

'Someone eats the moon,' said Reynard solemnly. 'We must find out who it is and stop them. Who could it be?'

Everybody thought hard. Then Long-ears the grey Rabbit, spoke.

'You know there is a rhyme about the cow jumping over the moon,' he said. 'Now why should a cow do such a thing? Why, to take a bite out of it as she jumps, of course!'

Also by Enid Blyton in Mammoth

Enid Blyton's
TEN MINUTE
TALES

MAMMOTH

First published 1934
by Methuen & Co Ltd
Published 1992 by Mammoth
an imprint of Reed Consumer Books Limited
Michelin House, 81 Fulham Road, London SW3 6RB
and Auckland, Melbourne, Singapore and Toronto

Reprinted 1992, 1993

Copyright © Enid Blyton 1934

Enid Blyton is a registered trademark of
Darrell Waters Ltd

ISBN 0 7497 1183 3

A CIP catalogue record for this title
is available from the British Library

Printed in Great Britain
by Cox & Wyman Ltd, Reading, Berkshire

CONTENTS

Mr Pipkin's Hat

MR PIPKIN was a round, fat little gnome, who wore big spectacles because he couldn't see very well. He lived with his old aunt, Mrs Pop-about, and she had brought him up since he was a tiny gnome of two years old.

Mrs Pop-about had quite spoilt Mr Pipkin. She never made him do anything he didn't want to, and he grew up with very bad manners. One thing especially annoyed the little folk of Hawthorn Town, and that was that Mr Pipkin always forgot to raise his hat when he met a lady.

Now, of course, every boy and every man raises his hat when he meets a lady, and when Mr Pipkin simply nodded his head and said good morning, without raising his hat even a quarter of a centimetre, well, everyone thought him very ill-mannered indeed. But no one quite liked to tell Mr Pipkin this, for although he was a merry little man, he had a hot temper.

Now one day there came a grand visitor to Hawthorn Town, no less a person than the cousin of the Fairy Queen herself, a very lovely and gracious lady. Everyone bowed low and pulled his hat right off his head when he met the lady riding or walking round town. It was really a great honour that she had come to stay there.

For some time Mr Pipkin didn't catch so much as a glimpse of the lady, and then one morning, when she was coming out of Mr Goodtart the baker's, he nearly bumped into her.

He stood back to let her pass, and nodded his head at her. He didn't bow or raise his hat, and the lady was very annoyed and astonished.

'The rude little man!' she thought. 'Surely he knows better manners than that! Does he *mean* to be rude to me, I wonder?'

She was so cross about it that she complained to Grey-beard, the chief of Hawthorn Town. He was very sorry to hear a complaint about anyone in his village, and he promised to set the matter right.

But when he came to think about it, and called a meeting, he didn't really see what could be done, except go to Mr Pipkin and tell him of his bad manners. And nobody would do that because of the little gnome's hot temper.

All the folk sat and thought for a while, and

then Chuckles, the smallest gnome there, jumped to his feet.

'*I* know what to do!' he cried. 'Let's send to the Wise Man on Breezy Hill and get an enchanted hat – one that will lift itself right off Mr Pipkin's head whenever he meets a lady! Then he'll *have* to learn manners, or he will keep losing his hat!'

'Splendid idea!' cried everyone, and they sent straightaway to the wise man for an enchanted hat. It came packed in a big box, and it *was* a lovely hat! The little folk had to pay ten silver pieces for it, but it was worth it.

It was bright red, and had a very tall crown. Round it was a band of yellow, and stuck in the band, right in the very front of the hat, was a great feather of blue. It really was a beautiful hat.

'We'll pack it up in its box again and send it through the post to Mr Pipkin,' said the gnomes. 'We won't say who has sent it, and he will think it is a present from someone.'

So next morning Mr Pipkin was most surprised to see the postman bringing him a big parcel; but he was more astonished still when he opened the box and found a beautiful feathered hat inside.

'My word!' he said. 'Here's a fine present! Who's it from?'

But there was no message in the box, and Mr Pipkin couldn't find out who had sent him such a wonderful present. He put the hat on his head and looked at himself in the glass.

'How fine I look!' he said. 'Why, it fits me as if it had been made for me! How everyone will envy me! I shall wear it this very morning.'

So out he went into the town, his new hat on his head, and very grand he felt. All the gnomes saw him, and nudged each other. So Mr Pipkin had got the hat safely then!

Now, it wasn't long before Mr Pipkin met Mother Muffin, doing her shopping. He nodded to her and said good morning – and at that very moment his new hat rose right off his head and flew to the ground. As soon as it reached the ground it grew a pair of little legs and started to run away.

'My!' said Mr Pipkin in astonishment, when he felt his hat go. 'What a wind there must be this morning, to be sure!'

He was too short-sighted to see the little legs that had grown from his new hat. He simply thought that the wind was blowing it along. He raced after it, puffing and blowing, and all the watching gnomes giggled and laughed till the tears ran down their faces.

At last Mr Pipkin caught his hat, and popped it on his head again, very firmly indeed. The little legs disappeared, and the hat behaved like an ordinary hat – but only until Mr Pipkin met Mrs Blue-Bonnet and her two daughters!

No sooner did they come in sight than off went that hat again, leaping from Mr Pipkin's head to the pavement. Then it grew its little legs and raced away once more.

Mr Pipkin was surprised and cross.

'Bother the wind!' he panted. 'Who would think it was so gusty! Why, I shouldn't have thought there was any breeze at all this morning!'

The hat gave him a good run that time, and the watching gnomes laughed till they had a stitch in their sides. Mr Pipkin caught the hat at last, dusted it, and popped it on to his head.

And at that very moment who should he meet but the grand lady again – and of course off went his hat at once, almost as soon as he had put it on again.

'Well, did you ever!' said Mr Pipkin, very much annoyed. 'This is a most extraordinary thing! What tricks the wind is playing this morning!'

Soon the word went round Hawthorn Town that Mr Pipkin's enchanted hat was having a fine game with him. All the little folk turned out to watch, and the young girl-gnomes made it their business to meet Mr Pipkin round every corner.

The little gnome couldn't think why his beautiful new hat flew from his head every second. He became very hot and tired chasing it, but he didn't like to let it go, for it was so very grand.

And then he suddenly noticed that his hat only flew off when he met a lady.

'That's a very funny thing,' said Mr Pipkin. 'The *next* time I meet a lady I'll hold you on very firmly, Hat!'

At that moment he met Susie Tips, and he clutched his hat hard. But it wasn't a bit of good – it flew off, giving his hand such a twist that he cried out in pain. Then it grew little legs again and raced down the street with Mr Pipkin after it.

When he picked it up, he saw little Chiffle-Chuffle the tailor nearby, and he spoke to him.

'I can't think what's the matter with my hat,' he said. 'It jumps off my head as soon as it sees a lady. I believe it's frightened of ladies – yes, that's what it must be!'

'Oh, *no*!' said Chiffle-Chuffle. 'It's an extra well-behaved hat, that's all, Mr Pipkin. Gentlemen always raise their hats when they

meet a lady, and perhaps you forgot to do that –
so your hat does it for you! Ha ha!'

Mr Pipkin stared at Chiffle-Chuffle, and went
very red. Of course! He quite well remembered
someone telling him that boys and men should
always raise their hats to ladies – but it had been
too much trouble, and he hadn't bothered about
his manners. And now he had a hat which had
better manners than he had. What a shocking
thing!

'Well, the only thing to do is to have good
manners myself,' said Mr Pipkin. 'I must raise
my hat politely to ladies, and then perhaps it
won't go rushing off like that.'

So when he met Dame Fiddle he raised his hat
as soon as ever he saw her, and the hat let him do
so, and allowed him to place it back firmly on his
head.

'Ho!' said Mr Pipkin. 'So that's it, is it? Well,
my manners need mending, that's certain, and if
I forget them this remarkable hat will remind
me!'

With that the fat little gnome laughed. He
walked all the way home and didn't forget to raise
his hat once, much to the astonishment of all the
folk of the town.

'He *has* learnt his lesson quickly!' they

whispered, and they admired him for it.

Well, from that very day Mr Pipkin's manners grew better and better. He became most polite and thoughtful, and soon the ladies had no fault to find with him at all.

But just now and then – not very often – Mr Pipkin forgets to raise his hat, and in a trice it leaps off his head, grows little legs, and rushes down the street at top speed! And if you suddenly see a hat do that you'll know who it is that is running after it – Mr Pipkin the gnome!

The Snippety Goblins

ONCE upon a time the Queen of Fairyland decided to have new curtains made for the whole of her palace. Now, as there were very nearly a thousand windows, you can guess that it was a great task to make enough new curtains for all the rooms.

'I don't quite know what to do,' said the Queen. 'If I get my sewing-maids to make the curtains it will take them *months*.'

'*I'll* tell you what to do!' said the King. 'Let me order you five hundred magic needles from the wizard who lives in Tiptoe Castle. He'll send them by coach, and all you need do is to have your curtains cut out ready, stick a needle into each one, say, "Needle, sew!" and each needle will make your curtain for you at once!'

'Oh, my dear, *do* order them for me!' cried the Queen in delight. 'Why, it wouldn't take a day to make the new curtains then! I should be so pleased.'

So the King sent an order to Tiptoe Castle, and the wizard promised to deliver the magic needles on the following Thursday when the coach ran between his castle and the King's palace.

Now who should get to hear of the load of needles but the Snippety Goblins, who lived in Cutaway Hill and spent all their time making clothes for pixies and elves!

'If only we could get hold of those needles we shouldn't have to work nearly so hard!' cried the goblin chief. 'We could just stick them into the clothes we were making, and say, "Needle, sew!" and in seconds the coats, tunics, and dresses would be made. What a lot of money we should make!'

'Can we get the needles?' asked the goblins eagerly.

'Well, they are coming by coach to the palace on Thursday,' said the chief goblin. 'Shall we lie in wait for it in Blackbird Wood, stop the horses, bind the driver, and then steal off with the sacks of needles?'

'Oh, yes!' cried the goblins. So they made all their plans, and when Thursday came they went to hide themselves in Blackbird Wood. Soon they heard the clip-clop of horses' hoofs, and down the woodland road came the coach carrying a load of magic needles, a batch of new-made cakes, six library books, and two passengers.

The goblins sprang to the horses' heads and stopped them. The chief goblin dragged the driver from his seat and bound him. Two other goblins bound the passengers to trees, and then the rest looked for the load of needles. They were in twelve sacks, and the goblins took them greedily.

'No one will find the driver and the passengers till late tonight,' said the goblins gleefully. 'By that time we shall be safely back in our hill, and no one will be able to take the needles from us!'

They set off through the wood, but they had forgotten the blackbirds that lived there in dozens. As soon as the goblins were out of sight the blackbirds flocked down to the coach and saw the driver and passengers bound with ropes.

'Some of you go to warn the King what has happened, and some of you fly after the goblins and keep them in sight!' cried the biggest blackbird, and the birds obeyed.

When the King heard what had happened he was full of rage. He ordered his soldiers out, and sent them after the robbers. Through Blackbird Wood they rode at top speed, and the blackbirds flew just in front, guiding them on their way.

For a long time the goblins did not know that they were being followed. They had come to a hill-side, and were lying down under a big bush to rest, for they were tired with carrying the needles, which were very heavy. Suddenly one goblin sat up and pointed.

'My goodness!' he cried. 'What's that!'

'It's the King's army after us!' cried the chief goblin, in a fright. 'Oh, whatever shall we do? If they catch us with the needles on us they will take us prisoners, and we shall be severely punished.'

'Let's hide them!' shouted the goblins.

'But where?' groaned the chief, looking all round. 'The hill-side is quite bare.'

'What about this bush?' called a goblin. 'Let's stick the needles into the leaves and pretend that it is a prickly bush. Then when the soldiers ride up we shall show them empty hands, and say we don't know anything at all about the needles.'

So every goblin worked hard, sticking the needles into the leaves of the tree, making it look as if it were a prickly bush. When all the needles had been hidden in this way, the goblins sat down again, pretending to be sleepy.

Soon the soldiers rode up and surrounded the tree.

'Ho, goblins, surrender!' cried the captain.

'You are robbers! You have stolen the King's needles!'

'Whatever do you mean?' cried the chief goblin, pretending to be most surprised. 'Why, we have no needles here at all! Come and look! We were just having a sleep under this bush.'

The soldiers dismounted and searched the goblins, but not a needle could they find. But they found something else that the goblins had forgotten all about – and that was the pile of sacks in which the needles had been packed.

'Ho!' cried the captain. 'It's no use telling untruths, goblins! Here are the sacks in which the needles were packed. Now quick – tell us where you have hidden them.'

But no goblin would say a word. At last, in a rage, the captain bade his men take hold of the little creatures and fling them into the bush under which they were sitting.

'No, no!' cried the goblins, remembering the needles hidden there. 'Mercy, mercy!'

But it was too late. Each goblin was swung into the bush, and, oh, dear me, how the needles pricked them! How they yelled and wept with rage and pain!

'Ooh, the needles are sticking into me!' each one cried, and the captain pricked up his ears. He looked closely at the leaves on the tree, and then shouted in surprise.

'Why, the cunning little creatures have stuck the magic needles all round the edges of this tree's leaves!' he cried. 'Ha ha, ho ho! What a shock for them when they were thrown among them! Well, they can stay there! The needles will keep them prisoner for many a long day.'

The captain rode off with his soldiers and told the King all that had happened.

'A good punishment for the robbers!' he said with a laugh. 'Let them get out of the tree as best they can. I must order a new load of needles for the Queen, for those in the bush will be of no use to her now. What about the tree? Does it mind having needles round its leaves?'

'Not at all, your Majesty,' said the captain, smiling. 'It has often complained that the cattle eat its leaves, but now, of course, no animal will touch it for fear of being pricked!'

'What is the tree called?' asked the King.

'It's a holly tree,' said the captain. And sure enough, a holly tree it was; and now you know how it is that it has such prickly leaves. Feel round the edge and you will find how sharp the needles are!

The goblins climbed out of the tree after a

time, but, oh, dear me, how scratched and pricked they were, and their fine clothes were all in ribbons! They stole back to their hill in shame, and never again did they steal anything. As for the holly tree, it was delighted, for no animal ever ate its leaves again!

The Talking Parrot

PRETTY POLL was a grey parrot who could say quite a number of things. She could say 'Good morning' and 'Good night', and never said them at the wrong times. She could whistle 'God save the Queen' and dance on her perch. She was really very clever.

She belonged to Timothy, a small boy who looked after her every day and loved her very much. He taught her all the words she knew, and she was very fond of him.

Polly could say, 'Dear, dear, I shall lose my train!' just like Daddy did at breakfast-time, and 'Bother it, I've dropped a stitch!' just like Mummy said when she was knitting. She could say, 'What are you doing?' in a very stern voice, exactly like Nanny's when she found Timothy being naughty.

When Timothy's little sister played hide-and-seek with Nanny, Polly watched in great excitement. Ann used to call 'I see you, I see you!' whenever she found Nanny, and soon Polly learnt to say it too. 'I see you, I see you!' she would call all day long.

When the time came for Timothy to go to boarding school, Mummy said that Polly had better be sold.

'I shan't have time to look after her,' Mummy said. 'I will look after your rabbits for you, and your pigeons, but I can't look after Polly, too.'

'Oh, Mummy!' cried Timothy in dismay. 'Please, *please*, don't sell my parrot! Oh, Mummy, you wouldn't, would you? I've taught her to talk so nicely, and I do love her so.'

'Well, darling, I really can't look after all your pets, and Baby too,' said Mummy. 'Besides, Polly does screech so, and makes such a dreadful noise.'

'Mummy, I shall be so unhappy if you sell Polly,' said Timothy, almost crying. 'Please don't.'

'Well, I'll see,' said Mummy, 'but I'm not going to promise anything, Timothy. If I hear of anyone who wants a parrot I think I shall have to let Polly go.'

Timothy was very sad. Polly was fond of him, and often climbed on to his shoulder and played with his ear. He did hope that Mummy wouldn't hear of anyone who wanted a parrot.

The day before Timothy was to go to school was not a very happy one. Timothy gave his rabbits an extra good feed and played with his four white pigeons all the morning. They were very tame and flew down to his hands whenever he called them. Bingo, his dog, went about with his tail down all day, for he somehow knew that Timothy was going away.

Polly guessed there was something happening too, and she screeched so much that Mummy said that dreadful bird really must be sent away. Timothy stopped Polly making a noise, and gave her a piece of apple to eat. He was very much afraid that when he came back from school Polly wouldn't be there.

That night Timothy couldn't get to sleep. He heard Mummy and Daddy go to bed, and he lay and listened to the quietness of the house. The wardrobe gave a creak, and an owl outside said 'Too-whoo-oo-oo-oo!' Timothy thought the night was very long.

Then suddenly he heard a queer noise, and he sat up in bed and listened. It sounded just like the kitchen window being opened! But who would open the window so late at night? Nanny was in bed long ago.

'Perhaps it's robbers,' thought Timothy in

excitement. 'I'll creep to the head of the stairs and see if I can hear anything more.'

He slipped out of bed and went quietly to the landing. He could hear nothing. Bingo was out in the yard, and he wasn't barking at all, so Timothy thought he couldn't have heard the kitchen window after all.

'I'll just pop downstairs and get myself an apple,' he thought. 'Then when I've eaten it, perhaps I shall go to sleep.'

So he crept quietly downstairs, and was just going into the dining room when he heard another noise. Timothy slipped behind the sofa. He peeped round the side, and by the moonlight that streamed through the window he saw two men.

'Burglars!' thought Timothy. 'How can I get upstairs to tell Daddy? I'm sure the men will see me if I move from here.'

Timothy didn't know what to do. He saw the men quietly taking the silver from the sideboard and rolling it in cloths so that it would not make a noise. They put it into a sack, and spoke to each other in whispers.

And then suddenly Polly the parrot woke up. She couldn't think what was happening, and scratched her head. The men could not see her, for she was in a dark corner. And suddenly she spoke very sternly.

'What are you doing?' she said. 'What are you doing?'

The men stopped in a fright and looked round the room to see who was speaking. But they could see no one at all.

'Did you hear that voice, Bill?' whispered one of the men.

'Yes, but I can't see anyone,' said the other.

'I see you, I see you!' said Polly, and then gave a most terrible screech. The men dropped their sack and ran for the window. They flung it open and jumped out into the garden below. They were terrified, for they did not know it was only Polly speaking.

Timothy ran to the window too, and watched the men go tearing down the street. Then he went to wake his father.

'Daddy, do come downstairs,' he said. 'Some burglars came tonight, and Polly frightened them away. Isn't she clever?'

Soon Daddy and Mummy ran downstairs to see what had happened.

'I see you, I see you!' said Polly. Then she whistled 'God Save the Queen', and did a little dance.

'Good old Polly,' said Daddy when he saw the sack of silver that the men had packed to take away. 'You've saved us a lot of money tonight! Come along, you must go back to bed, Timothy. You've got to go to school tomorrow, remember.'

'Good night, good night. I've dropped a stitch!' called Polly, as they all went upstairs.

'Mummy, you won't send my Polly away now she's been so clever, will you?' said Timothy, as he got into bed. Mummy kissed him and tucked him up.

'Oh, no, darling,' she said. 'Polly shall certainly stay with us. I wouldn't think of selling her now! So go to sleep and don't worry about her any more!'

Timothy smiled in delight and then fell fast asleep. Polly was fast asleep too, happy because everyone had petted her.

As for the robbers, a policeman caught them, and they were punished; but to the end of their lives they never guessed that it was only a parrot who had scared them away that night!

The Fox and the Six Cats

THERE were once six cats who all belonged to an old lady called Miss Two-Shoes. There was a brown cat, a black cat, a white one, a ginger one, a tabby one, and one that was every colour mixed.

Every day for their dinner Miss Two-Shoes put out six dishes of boiled fish and milk. The cats loved fish, and ate their dinners hungrily, always wishing for more.

'If only we knew where these fish come from, we might be able to go and get some,' said the black cat, cleaning her whiskers carefully.

'*I* know where they live!' said the ginger cat. 'They live in the river that runs in the field at the bottom of our garden! Last night, when I was prowling about there, I saw a man with a long rod and line. He threw the line into the river, and very soon, when he pulled it out again, there was a wriggling fish on the end.'

'Ho!' said the white cat, yawning widely. 'So that's where the fish come from, is it? Well, I don't see how we can catch any, unless we have a rod and line ourselves!'

All the cats had listened to what the ginger cat had said, and each had made up his mind that he would go that night, all by himself, and watch the fisherman at work.

So when night fell all the cats started off for the river, and none of them saw each other, for they trod so quietly on their velvet paws.

The fisherman was there. He had baited his line, and was just casting it into the wide river. Then he felt in his pocket for his pipe, for he loved to smoke whilst he was waiting in the moonlight for the fish to bite. But he had left his pipe in his cottage at the other end of the field.

'Bother!' he said crossly. 'I must either go without my smoke or walk back to my cottage. Well, I will balance my rod carefully here, and go quickly to fetch my pipe. I don't suppose any fish will bite yet.'

He put his rod down and set off to walk to his cottage; and, do you know, he had hardly taken ten steps before a big fish snapped at the bait! The hook stuck into his mouth and it was caught!

Then it began to wriggle and struggle, and the six watching cats suddenly saw it jumping in and out of the water. Each of them darted forward to take the fish, and how cross they were when they saw the others!

'Quick!' said the black cat, pouncing on the rod and holding it. 'One of you reel in the line.'

The ginger cat wound in the line and pulled the fish nearer. The white cat fetched the landing-net to catch the fish in. The tabby helped to hold it, whilst the brown cat shouted directions all the time. The sixth cat ran to each in turn, giving a paw here and a paw there. They were all as excited as could be.

The fish pulled hard. The rod bent nearly in two. The black cat found it quite difficult to hold, and was half afraid she would be pulled into the water.

The ginger cat wound the line in steadily, and the fish was pulled nearer and nearer to the bank. Then the white cat and the tabby tried to put the landing-net over it, and very soon they managed to. The fish was caught! It slipped into the net, the cats lifted it ashore, and the big fish lay shining in the moonlight.

'The fish is mine!' said the black cat. 'I held the rod!'

'No, it's mine!' said the ginger one. 'I reeled in the line!'

'Well, I fetched the landing-net!' said the white cat.

'And I helped to hold it!' said the tabby.

'I told you all what to do!' said the brown cat.

'And I helped everyone in turn,' said the sixth one. 'Besides, I'm sure I saw the fish first. It should be mine.'

Then they all began to quarrel hard, and a fox, who was passing that way, heard them, and came to see what was the matter. When he saw the big fish lying there he was pleased, and made up his mind to get it for himself.

'Now, what's the matter?' he asked. 'Come, come, do not make this noise.'

'We each of us want the fish,' said the black cat. 'We don't know who should have it.'

'Well, I will be your judge,' said the fox. 'Now, I have heard that you all have beautiful voices, and often sing to the moon. I will hear you all sing, and then whichever of you has the loveliest voice shall have the fish.'

The cats agreed, for each secretly thought that his own voice was far the best.

'Very well,' said the sly fox. 'Now I will hear you all together. Sit up straight, fix your eyes on the moon, and sing your most beautiful song to her for two minutes without stopping. Don't take your eyes from the moon or that will count a mark against you.'

The cats all sat up straight, looked up at the moon and began to caterwaul. Oh, what a fearful noise it was! The fox thought it was dreadful; but did he wait to judge the singing? Not he! All the cats were looking hard at the moon and saw nothing but that, so the artful fox quietly picked up the fish and ran off with it, chuckling to himself as he heard the ugly song behind him.

For quite three minutes the cats sang their best, and then, becoming tired, they looked down to ask the fox which of them had won. But he wasn't there! Nor was the fish!

'Oh, the scoundrel! Oh, the rascal! Oh, the scamp!' cried all the cats angrily. 'He has stolen the fish from us!'

Then, oh, dear me! The fisherman returned, and when he found the six cats howling dismally, and his rod and line all disarranged, he *was* angry! He sent them mewing away.

'If only we had been sensible and shared the big fish between us we should be eating it now!' said the black cat. 'How silly we are!'

And they were, weren't they?

Hee-Haw and the Lions

ONCE Hee-Haw the Donkey stood munching by a hedge, listening to what Farmer Giles was saying to his wife. Suddenly he pricked up his ears and stopped eating, in a fright.

Then he galloped off to where Nanny the Goat was standing by a gorse-bush.

'Nanny-Goat!' he cried. 'I have dreadful news for you. Take your little ones to safety, for Farmer Giles says there are lions about in the fields!'

'My goodness!' said Nanny in a fright. 'I must go and tell Moo the Cow. She has two dear little calves.'

Off she ran to Moo the Cow, who was lying down with her calves in the field.

'Moo!' she cried, 'I have dreadful news for you. Take your little ones to safety, for Hee-Haw the Donkey says there are lions about in the fields!'

'Great buttercups!' said Moo the Cow, getting up in a hurry. 'I must go and tell Dobbin the

Horse. She has a dear little foal.' Off she went to where Dobbin was lying with her foal.

'Dobbin!' she cried. 'I have dreadful news for you. Take your little one to safety, for Nanny the Goat says there are lions about in the fields!'

'Tails and whiskers!' said Dobbin the Horse, swishing her great tail from side to side. 'I must go and tell Dilly the Duck. She has ten dear little ducklings.'

Off she galloped to Dilly the Duck, who was swimming on the pond with her ten yellow ducklings.

'Dilly!' she cried. 'I have dreadful news for you. Take your little ones to safety, for Moo the Cow says there are lions about in the fields!'

'Feathers and fluff!' cried Dilly the Duck, waddling off the water in a hurry. 'I must go and tell Cluck the Hen. She has seven dear little chicks.'

Off she waddled to where Cluck the Hen was pecking in the yard with her seven chicks.

'Cluck!' cried Dilly. 'I have dreadful news for you. Take your little ones to safety, for Dobbin the Horse says there are lions about in the fields!'

'Beaks and tails!' cried Cluck the Hen. 'I must go and tell Jenny the Dog. She has three dear little puppies.'

Off she ran to Jenny the Dog, who was lying in her kennel with her puppies round her.

'Jenny!' cried Cluck. 'I have dreadful news for you. Take your little ones to safety, for Dilly the Duck says there are lions about in the fields!'

'Sniffs and wags!' cried Jenny the Dog. 'I must go and tell Mrs Giles, the farmer's wife. She has two dear little children.'

Off she scampered to where Mrs Giles was skimming cream in the dairy, her two children playing nearby.

'Mrs Giles!' cried Jenny. 'I have dreadful news for you. Take your little ones to safety, for Cluck the Hen says there are lions about in the fields!'

Mrs Giles laughed.

'Cluck is playing a joke on you!' she said. 'I am sure there are no lions about. I will go and see what Cluck means.'

So Jenny the Dog and Mrs Giles went to where Cluck the Hen was running into the hen-house with all her little chicks.

'Who told you there were lions in the fields?' asked Mrs Giles.

'Dilly the Duck!' answered Cluck. 'Why, aren't there any?'

'No!' said Mrs Giles. 'Let us go and see what Dilly the Duck means.'

So Mrs Giles, Jenny the Dog, and Cluck the Hen went to where Dilly the Duck was hiding under a bush with her ten ducklings round her.

'Who told you there were lions in the fields?' asked Mrs Giles.

'Dobbin the Horse!' answered Dilly. 'Why, aren't there any?'

'No!' said Mrs Giles. 'Let us go and see what Dobbin the Horse means.'

So Mrs Giles, Jenny the Dog, Cluck the Hen, and Dilly the Duck went to where Dobbin the Horse was standing safely in her stable with her foal.

'Who told you there were lions about in the fields?' asked Mrs Giles.

'Moo the Cow!' answered Dobbin. 'Why, aren't there any?

'No!' said Mrs Giles. 'Let us go and see what Moo the Cow means.'

So Mrs Giles, Jenny the Dog, Cluck the Hen, Dilly the Duck, and Dobbin the Horse went to where Moo the Cow was hiding under a hedge with her two calves.

'Who told you there were lions in the fields?' asked Mrs Giles.

'Nanny the Goat,' answered Moo. 'Why, aren't there any?'

'No!' said Mrs Giles. 'Let us go and see what Nanny the Goat means.'

So Mrs Giles, Jenny the Dog, Cluck the Hen, Dilly the Duck, Dobbin the Horse, and Moo the Cow went to where Nanny the Goat was hiding under a gorse bush with her little kids.

'Who told you there were lions in the fields?' asked Mrs Giles.

'Hee-Haw the Donkey,' said Nanny-Goat. 'Why, aren't there any?'

'No!' said Mrs Giles. 'Let us go and see what Hee-Haw the Donkey means.'

So Mrs Giles, Jenny the Dog, Cluck the Hen, Dilly the Duck, Dobbin the Horse, Moo the Cow, and Nanny the Goat went to where Hee-Haw the Donkey was standing trembling by the gate.

'Who told you there were lions in the fields?' asked Mrs Giles.

'Why, Mrs Giles!' cried Hee-Haw in surprise. 'It was Mr Giles I heard telling *you* not so very long ago when you were standing by this gate here.'

Then Mrs Giles began to laugh and laugh.

'Oh, you *are* a silly donkey!' she cried. 'Why, Farmer Giles said what a dreadful lot of *dandelions* there were in the fields! Don't you know what *dandelions* are?'

Then Hee-Haw the donkey hung his head and looked quite ashamed of himself. All the animals laughed at him, and went away to tell the young ones that there was nothing to be frightened of after all.

And now whenever Moo the Cow or any of the others meets Hee-Haw they always ask him the same question:

'Have you seen any lions about today, Hee-Haw?' And you should just hear them laugh when Hee-Haw the Donkey gallops away in a temper!

The Dog Whose Tail Wouldn't Wag

THERE was once a very lazy, good-for-nothing dog called Paddy who lay in the sun all day and yawned. He was a miserable fellow, for he never went for a walk, never said 'How-do-you-do?' to another dog, and wouldn't trouble himself to bark even when the dirtiest tramp came begging.

And one day he found that he had lost the wag in his tail! It simply *wouldn't* wag, no matter how hard he tried to make it. Paddy was very much upset about it, because a dog who cannot wag his tail is a funny fellow to see, and everyone laughed at him.

'You'll have to get the wag back into your tail somehow,' said his friend Rover to him. 'It is a silly thing to see a tail without a wag. Why, how is any dog to know if you are friendly or not if you can't wag your tail? Everyone will be fighting you, and you won't like that at all!'

Paddy didn't know *what* to do! At last he made up his mind to go and see Mother Hubble, who was half a witch, and could perhaps give him something to put the wag back into his tail. So off he went and told her his trouble.

'Well, I've a spell here that will do the trick,' said Mother Hubble. 'But you must catch me a rabbit for my dinner if you want it.'

Paddy ran off. He found it very hard work indeed to catch a rabbit; for he had been lazy for so long that he had forgotten how to set to work. But at last he caught one, and carried it to Mother Hubble for her dinner.

She gave him the spell wrapped up in a bit of paper.

'Be careful not to drop it,' she said. 'It is a yellow powder.'

Paddy took it in his mouth and set off home. But on the way he yawned so widely that the parcel fell from his mouth and came undone. In a flash the wind whipped up the powder, and blew most of it into the trees. Ever since then their leaves and twigs have wagged in the breeze and hardly ever stop.

A few grains of the spell blew on to Paddy's whiskers, and, oh, my goodness, they began to wag like mad! Paddy felt them wagging to and fro, and he couldn't stop them!

How everyone laughed at him! It was too funny to see a dog with wagging whiskers. Paddy was ashamed and hid himself away; but soon he could bear it no longer, and off he went to the witch again. She soon took the wag out of his whiskers, but how she laughed at him!

'Well, you shall have another spell, but you must hunt me up a basketful of mushrooms,' she said.

So Paddy took a basket and went to hunt for mushrooms. It *was* hard work, and he grew very tired. Up and down the fields he went, and at last, after a long morning's work, he had filled the basket. He took it to Mother Hubble, and she gave him another wag-spell wrapped up in a piece of paper.

'Now be careful of it this time!' she said.

He set off home, but he was so tired after hunting for mushrooms that he hadn't gone very far before he yawned again, even more widely than before. Out dropped the parcel from his mouth and the wind whipped up the powder again. Most of it blew on to a little black and white bird nearby, and it began wagging its tail like mad. It has done so ever since, and you must often have seen it, for wagtails are quite common.

Some of the powder blew on to Paddy's ears, and they began to wag too. How they wagged! One wagged forwards and back and the other wagged from side to side. He was the funniest sight to see, and it was no wonder that everyone stood still and laughed at him.

'Oh, my!' thought Paddy, running off in shame. 'What an unlucky dog I am! First my whiskers wagged and now my ears! Perhaps the spell will wear off!'

But it didn't, and very soon Paddy was forced to go to Mother Hubble again, for he was so tired of being laughed at.

She put his ears right for him, and laughed merrily.

'I suppose you want *another* wag-spell!' she said. 'Well, I'd better give you twice as much powder this time, for you waste so much each time that even if you did get home with this spell and used it you would probably have wasted such a lot on the way that your tail would only make a very feeble wag. Go and dig me up some potatoes, and I will give you another wag-spell.'

All that day Paddy dug up potatoes with his paws, and didn't he get tired! When he had finished, the witch gave him another wag-spell wrapped up in a piece of paper, and warned him solemnly not to yawn till he got home.

Well, Paddy actually managed to remember not to, and he got home with the parcel of yellow

powder safely in his mouth. He asked his friend
Rover to come in and rub it all into his tail, and he
quite forgot that the witch had given him twice as
much as he needed!

His tail began to wag very fast, and because
there was so much wag-powder on it Paddy
couldn't stop it wagging! It wagged up and down
and to and fro, and Paddy turned his head round
and watched it in dismay.

'This is as bad as not being able to wag it at all!'
he said to Rover. 'Goodness me, why won't it
stop? Just look at it wagging there as if it were the
pendulum of a clock!'

Paddy soon became very tired of having a tail
that never stopped wagging, for he couldn't even
go to sleep without being woken up by its wag-
wag-wag. So back he went to Mother Hubble
again.

'Well, Paddy,' she said, 'the reason that you
lost your wag in the beginning was because you
were such a lazy, good-for-nothing, miserable
little dog who never did a day's work for anyone.
Come and work for me for a month and your tail
will get all right again by itself. Happy, hard-
working dogs never have any bother with their
wags.'

So Paddy went to work for Mother Hubble for

a month, and how he worked, too! He fetched
and carried for her, he learnt to pump the water
with his front paws, he guarded the house and he
barked at tramps and burglars. He soon found
that hard work and happiness go together, and
one day, to his great joy, he saw that his tail was
quite all right again.

'It wags when I want it to, and it keeps still
when I want it to!' he told the witch joyfully. 'It is
quite cured.'

'I'm very glad,' said Mother Hubble, patting
him. 'Well, your month is up, and you may go
now. But don't forget that if you want to keep
your wag you mustn't be afraid of hard work!'

'I don't want to go,' said Paddy. 'I am happy in
working for you, and if you'll let me stay I'll be
your dog and look after you.'

So he stayed with Mother Hubble, and as far as
I know he is with her still, and his tail has never
again lost its cheerful wag-wag-wag.

The Big Bouncing Ball

IN a shop sat a big bouncing ball. It was red, yellow, blue, and green, and it was very proud of itself indeed.

'Ho!' it said to the other toys. 'I am a grand fellow, I am! I shall be bought by a rich man's child, and put into a grand nursery! You'll see! I shall be much too grand to talk to any of you if I meet you out!'

'How you do talk!' said the brown Teddy bear. 'Pride comes before a fall. Be careful!'

'I'm tired of listening to you,' said the baby doll.

'So am I,' said the little wooden horse.

But the ball took no notice, and went on boasting loudly.

At that moment the shop door opened, and in came a beautifully-dressed child, a little girl with long, golden hair down her back. Her nanny was with her, and they looked all round the shop.

'I want a ball,' said the little girl. 'A very beautiful ball. Look! There's one up there!'

She pointed to the big bouncing ball, and it swelled with pride.

'What did I tell you?' it whispered to the others.

The little girl bought it, and carried it out of the shop under her arm. How proud the ball was!

'I shall be the nicest toy in the nursery!' it said to itself. 'I shall be this little girl's favourite toy! Oh, what a grand fellow I shall become!'

But just then the little girl took out the ball from under her arm and looked at it.

'Nanny,' she said, 'this ball isn't as pretty as I thought. I wonder if it is a good bouncer.'

She bounced it, and the ball was so anxious to show what it could do that it bounced as high as it could and hit the little girl on the nose.

Then what a temper she was in! She took the ball in her right hand and flung it away from her.

'You horrid, nasty thing!' she cried. 'I don't want you! You hit me on the nose. Go away, you ugly, common ball!'

The ball rolled away in dismay. It was on a hill, and it couldn't stop rolling. On it went, and on and on, rolling into puddles and out again, rolling into mud and getting smudged and dirty.

'Oh, what a nasty little girl!' it thought. 'Fancy throwing away a beautiful ball like me! Oh, whatever shall I do now?'

It rolled to the bottom of the hill and lay there. Then there came by a big dog and sniffed at it. He picked it up in his mouth and ran off with it. How frightened the ball was! The dog threw it into the air, and when it bumped to the ground and rolled away he ran after it and picked it up again.

Then he began chewing it, and he chewed a big hole in one side. The ball tried its hardest to roll away, but it couldn't.

Then the dog picked it up again and ran off with it. He carried it until he came to a stream, and then he wanted a drink. So he dropped the ball into the water and began to drink.

The ball was carried away on the stream. It felt more frightened than ever. It had never seen water before, and it felt very cold and strange. Also its colour was beginning to come off, and the ball felt dirty and old, although it had only been bought that very morning.

For hours the water took the ball along, and soon the stream grew deeper and wider, and became a river. Still the ball floated along, though now it felt heavier, because the water was beginning to leak into the hole that the dog had made, and the inside was slowly filling up.

'Then I shall sink and drown!' thought the

poor ball in a fright. 'Oh, how I wish I was back in the shop again with the Teddy bear, the baby doll and the wooden horse. How I wish I hadn't boasted so often! The bear warned me that pride came before a fall!'

At last, just before it grew dark, the ball came to a very dirty part of the river. Tall, sooty buildings stood on either side, and ragged little children played by the edge of the water. The ball bumped against the side of the river, and wondered when it would sink, for it felt very full of water.

'Oh!' suddenly cried a child's voice. 'Look! There's a lovely ball! Let's get it out of the water and play with it!'

The children fished the poor sodden ball out of the river, squeezed the water from it, and wiped it dry. All the lovely colours were gone, there was a hole in one side, and the ball looked very odd indeed.

But the ragged little children thought it was beautiful.

'Ooh! Isn't it a big one!' they cried. 'Let's bounce it!'

The ball hadn't much bounce left, but it was so grateful to be played with that it did its best, and the children shouted for joy.

'It shall be our nicest toy!' they said. 'We will keep it carefully and play with it every day!'

So they did, and the ball was very happy, for the children loved it. Then one day, when one of the boys was playing with it in the park, the ball saw the Teddy bear sitting on the knee of a little girl nearby.

'Good gracious!' said the Teddy bear, in a scornful voice. 'Can this really be the wonderful ball I used to know? Ah, well, I always told you that pride came before a fall!'

But the ball only laughed. It was happy to please the little ragged children, and it had no more pride left.

'I was beautiful in the old days, and nobody loved me,' said the ball. 'But I am ugly now, and all the children are fond of me.'

And it gave an extra big bounce that made all the boys and girls shout with delight!

Buttercup and the Moon

ONCE upon a time Reynard the Fox and Sharp-eye the Weasel looked up into the sky and noticed that the moon was only half a moon.

'It was a big round moon not so many nights ago,' said Reynard. 'It was fine to hunt by because it gave so much light. What has happened to it?'

'It keeps going like that,' said Sharp-eye the Weasel. 'Sometimes it is big and round and sometimes it is little and curved.'

'Now why should that be?' said Reynard. 'It would be far better for our hunting if the moon was always big and round. We should see much better.'

'Perhaps someone eats bits out of the moon,' said Sharp-eye. 'I have heard that it is made of green cheese, and it might easily be that someone bites pieces out of it now and again.'

'You may be right,' said Reynard. 'Let us call a meeting and find out who eats the moon.'

So they called a meeting and all the animals

came – the rabbit, the hare, the mole, the stoat, the hedgehog, and the bat.

'Someone eats the moon,' said Reynard solemnly. 'We must find out who it is and stop them. Who could it be?'

Everybody thought hard. Then Long-ears the grey Rabbit, spoke.

'You know there is a rhyme about the cow jumping over the moon,' he said. 'Now why should a cow do such a thing? Why, to take a bite out of it as she jumps, of course!'

Everyone clapped at this. They thought it was a very good guess.

'You must be right,' said Reynard. 'I will see the cow about it.'

'We will come with you,' said all the animals. So off they went to the field where Buttercup, the old brown cow, was lying down asleep. She was surprised to find such a crowd round her when she awoke.

'What do you want?' she asked.

'We want to know why you keep eating the moon,' said Reynard sternly.

'Whatever do you mean?' asked Buttercup in astonishment. 'Eat the moon! Whatever next? Why, I have plenty of sweet grass without bothering about a silly thing like the moon!'

'We don't believe you,' said Reynard. 'Listen, Buttercup! If you eat the moon any more we will chain you up in a dark shed and you will not be allowed on the sunny hill-side again.'

The cow tossed her head and flicked her tail at the fox.

'Silly creature!' she said. 'Go away. I tell you I *don't* eat the moon.'

'Well, remember we have warned you!' said Reynard, and he and all the animals went away.

Now the next night was cloudy and the moon only showed itself once, then it disappeared. The animals felt certain that Buttercup had jumped up into the sky and eaten up every bit of the moon. They were angry, for they thought that if the moon was eaten all up it would never grow again.

'Fetch a chain and we will tie up the cow in a shed,' said Reynard. 'Then she can do no more damage. She will eat the stars next, the greedy creature.'

So a strong chain was fetched and they all set off for Buttercup's field. They put the chain round her neck, and made her walk down the hill until she came to a dark shed. They took her inside and chained her up.

'Now you can do no more harm!' they said.

'Leave the sky alone, you wicked cow. You have eaten the moon all up and we shall never see it again.'

The poor cow wept and sighed, but it was of no use. She could not get free, so she had to lie down and make the best of things. But how she missed the windy hill-side and the sweet green grass!

For a long time the weather was rainy, and clouds covered the sky. Not once did the moon shine, and the animals sorrowed to think that it should all be eaten.

'We will have the cow out tonight, and decide what to do to punish her for such a dreadful deed,' said Reynard. So that night Buttercup was taken out of the shed, and set in the middle of a ring with all the animals sitting round her. She was very sad and hung her big brown head.

'Now,' said Reynard, standing up, 'we have come here to decide what punishment to give the prisoner for daring to eat our lovely moon. Never more will it shine down to give us light – the greedy cow you see before you has gobbled it all up!'

And then, at that very moment the silver moon sailed out from behind a cloud and shone down on all the animals below! She was quite full, very round and very bright, and she seemed to smile at everyone.

'Look!' said the cow. 'There is the moon! Why do you say I have eaten her? You are very unkind to me. I wouldn't do any harm to such a beautiful thing. If I had eaten her she wouldn't be in the sky, would she?'

All the animals went red and looked at one another. The cow was quite right. She could not have eaten the moon if it was still in the sky. What a strange thing!

'You are free,' said Reynard, and he took the chain from Buttercup's neck. She ran off to her field, mooing gladly, and began to nibble the green grass in delight.

'The moon is a mystery,' said Long-ears the Rabbit. 'Let us be thankful we have it, whether large or small, round or like a slice of melon. She comes when she will, we none of us know why!'

'There is a book in the schoolroom down in the village which tells all about the moon,' said Prickles the Hedgehog.

'Who can read?' asked Reynard. But nobody could, and one by one all the animals slipped away. Reynard was left alone, looking up at the silver moon. She seemed to laugh at him, and he grew angry.

'I'll eat you myself! I'll eat you myself!' he cried. He leapt high into the air, but he could not reach the moon. He jumped again, but it was no use – the moon sailed in the sky, and took no notice of him at all.

'Moo moo!' suddenly said Buttercup, looking over the hedge. 'So *you're* the one that jumps at the moon and nibbles it, are you? Moo moo!'

Then Reynard ran away as fast as his four legs would take him, and he never dared to go near Buttercup again, in case she told tales of him. But it would have served him right if she had, wouldn't it?

The Enchanted Spade

THERE was once a brownie called Hum who had a big garden. He was very lazy, and when the time came for him to dig his kitchen garden from top to bottom he felt as if he really couldn't do it.

'You should buy one of those dig-away spades,' said Gillie, a friend of his. 'All you do is to stick the spade in your garden and say, "Dig away, dig away!" and it digs all by itself.'

'Ooh!' said Hum, quite excited. 'That sounds fine. Where can I get one, and how much are they?'

'Mother Chinky sells them, away up on Blowaway Hill,' said Gillie. 'But they are very expensive, so I don't expect you will be able to buy one.'

'I'll go and find out,' said Hum. So off he went. It took him an hour to get to Mother Chinky's, and when he got there he saw all the dig-away spades neatly set out in a row in the garden. Mother Chinky was at her front door, knitting.

'Good morning,' said Hum. 'How much are the dig-away spades?'

'Ten gold pieces each,' said Mother Chinky.

'Ooh!' said Hum. 'I've not even got *one*. Would you just lend me a spade, Mother Chinky?'

'No, indeed I won't,' said the old woman crossly. 'I've heard you are very lazy, and it won't hurt you at all to dig your garden yourself, Hum, with an ordinary spade. Go away!'

Hum turned away sulkily. Just at that moment up came Mr Biggity, the gnome. He was a big and powerful fellow, and he asked Mother Chinky if she had a dig-away spade big enough for him.

'I'm afraid I haven't,' said Mother Chinky. 'But bring me your own spade, Biggity, and I'll soon turn it into a dig-away one.'

Now as soon as Hum heard her say this he made up his mind to hide behind the wall until Biggity fetched his own spade. Then he would see what Mother Chinky did to make it a magic one. After that he would run home and turn his own spade into a dig-away one. Oh, that was a fine plan, thought Hum.

Mr Biggity soon came back, carrying his own large spade. Mother Chinky stuck it into the ground, and danced round it three times. Then she clapped it twice on the handle and said:

> 'Dig away, spade,
> With your strong steel blade,
> Dig in the ground,
> Make never a sound.
> Dig away, dig away, spade'

'Thank you, Mother Chinky,' said Biggity, and he went off with the spade over his shoulder. Hum stole away too, delighted to think that he knew the spell to make a dig-away spade.

As soon as he got home he fetched his spade and stuck it into the ground. Then he danced round it three times, clapped it twice on the handle, and said the magic rhyme:

> 'Dig away, spade,
> With your strong steel blade,
> Dig in the ground,
> Make never a sound.
> Dig away, dig away, spade'

At once his spade began to dig all by itself. It was wonderful to see it. It delved deep into the earth, threw up the clods, and dug down deep again. It worked in a straight row, and Hum stood and watched it in delight. Soon it finished the first row and started on the next.

Hum went indoors to cook his dinner. After a while he looked out of the window. The dig-away spade had finished digging all the kitchen garden, and was now digging in the rose garden!

'Hey, stop!' shouted Hum, rushing into the garden. 'Don't dig there, stupid spade! You'll dig up all my roses! Keep to the kitchen garden. Dig it over again, if you want some more work to do!'

But the spade wouldn't stop. It dug up a beautiful rose tree and sent it flying in the air. Then it dug up another. Hum couldn't bear it. He rushed to the spade, and tried to take it away from his roses. But the spade gave him such a blow on his toes that he ran away howling in pain.

'Oh, oh!' he cried. 'It's hurt me; it's hurt me! Stop, you nasty spade, stop!'

But the spade simply would *not* stop. It dug up each of the rose trees, and then started on the daffodil bulbs that were just beginning to send up tall green leaves. Hum cried with rage, but it wasn't a bit of good. He couldn't make the spade stop, and he didn't dare to go near it again in case it dug him on the toes.

After the dig-away spade had dug up all the

bulbs it began to dig up the garden fence! Oh, what a dreadful thing to do! Hum called to it to stop, he begged it to stop, and he wept with big tears, but the spade took no notice at all.

'It'll dig my house up next!' wept Hum. 'There's only one thing to do – I must go and fetch Mother Chinky!'

Off he ran to Mother Chinky, and wasn't she surprised to see him! When she heard what had happened she began to laugh – and she laughed and she laughed and she laughed.

'Oh, dear, oh, dear!' she said. 'This is the best joke I've heard for years! Fancy you putting the dig-away spell on your spade, and not bothering to find out how to make it stop digging! Well, it will certainly dig up your house, Hum!'

'Oh, don't laugh any more!' begged Hum. 'Do, do tell me how to stop it. I'm dreadfully sorry I took the spell without asking you, now, and I'll do anything you like if only you'll tell me how to stop the spade from digging any more.'

'Well, if I tell you that, you can just come to me every Monday and do my washing for two months,' said Mother Chinky. 'I've a nasty pain in my back, and can't stoop over my wash-tub as I used to. And you're so lazy that it will be good for you to have some hard work to do for once!'

'I'll do it for you,' promised Hum. 'But do quickly tell me how to stop the spade digging.'

'Well, all you've got to do is to clap your hands twice and say:

> "Rest, spade, rest.
> You've done your very best," '

said Mother Chinky.

Hum raced off down the hill as fast as he could go. When he got home he found that every plant in his garden had been dug up, his fence was lying flat on the ground, and the spade was just digging up his tool-shed.

He clapped his hands twice and shouted:

> 'Rest, spade, rest.
> You've done your very best.'

At once the spade stopped working, and stood quite still in the ground. Hum groaned when he looked at all the damage that had been done.

'Instead of saving me work that horrid spade has made enough work to keep me busy for weeks!' sighed Hum. 'There are all those plants and rose trees to put back, the fence to put up again, and the tool-shed to mend. And I've got to go and do Mother Chinky's washing too! Well, I'll never be lazy again, if I can help it!'

And, so Mother Chinky says, Hum has turned over quite a new leaf, and works as hard as anybody now. You should just see how well he does her washing every Monday!

The Swallow that was Left Behind

THERE was once a young swallow that had a very happy time in our land all through the summer. When the cold days came the old swallows called him.

'Little-wings, you must come with us,' they said. 'We are gathering together ready to fly from here to a warm country far away.'

'But I don't want to go away from here!' cried Little-wings. 'Let me stay a little longer.'

'No,' said the old birds. 'You must come. Soon there will be no insects for you to eat here, and you will starve if you stay.'

'How do you know?' asked Little-wings, rudely. 'If you never stay for the winter, you don't know what it is like, do you? The freckled thrush stays, and the little robin. Why can't I stay too?'

'Because swallows never do,' answered the old birds patiently. 'Come with us, and do as you're told.'

Little-wings thought he knew better. He

didn't want to fly from the land he knew, far away over the sea to a strange country.

'I should get very tired,' he said to himself. 'I shall stay here. I will hide myself away till all the rest have gone.'

He found a thick ivy-grown wall, and hid under the leaves. He watched all the swallows gathering together on the telegraph wires and on the roof of the old barn. There were hundreds of them, twittering excitedly. They knew that it was time to go, for the cold north wind was blowing strongly. Little-wings heard them talking, and laughed to think that they would go without him.

One evening they flew. Every swallow rose in the air, and flew steadily southwards to where the sea gleamed blue. The strong north wind blew behind them, and soon they were out of sight. Little-wings was the only swallow left in England.

The next few days were sunny and warm, and Little-wings enjoyed himself very much. He made friends with a robin, and caught quite a lot of flies that danced in the sunshine. But the nights were cold, and Little-wings shivered, and wished he had a few more feathers.

When November came the days were foggy

and wet. Little-wings found that flies were getting fewer and fewer. The robin didn't want him and drove him away.

'There are not enough insects for you in this garden,' said he. 'Go somewhere else.'

But wherever he went there seemed to be a robin who said the same thing.

'In the winter we each take a beat of our own,' said one. 'We don't allow anyone else there, for then there would not be enough food. Go away!'

Little-wings was cold, lonely, and hungry. How he wished he had gone with the other swallows when he had the chance!

'I was young and foolish,' he thought. 'Oh, what shall I do? I shall soon die of cold, and when the others come back in the warm springtime I shall not be here to greet them!'

When snow and frost came the little swallow was nearly frozen. He was only skin and bone, for he had had nothing to eat for days. There were no flies to be found at all. Even the robins had to go and beg for crumbs at back doors.

He sat huddled up on a frosty post, feeling very cold and ill. Suddenly he heard a voice nearby.

'Why, look! Here's a little swallow! It didn't fly off with the others in the autumn! Oh,

Mummy, poor little thing, it's nothing but skin and feathers! Let's take it home and put it with our other birds.'

Then Little-wings felt himself gently picked up and carried into a warm house. He was put into a great big cage where many other little birds flew and chirruped gaily. They were foreign ones, and Little-wings did not understand their language, but he knew they were friendly.

The little girl who had rescued him gave him food. It was warm in the cage, and soon the little swallow felt better. In a day to two he was flying about merrily with the others, thankful that he was not in the cold world outside.

There he stayed, happy and well-cared for till the warm spring days came. Then the little girl took him from the cage and set him free.

'Your brothers and sisters will soon be back!' she cried. 'Go and welcome them.'

He flew off into the sunshine, and that very day the first swallows came back to England. They were tired after their long journey, and Little-wings gave them a warm welcome. He told them how foolish he had been, and how the little girl had rescued him.

'We'll all build in the barn near her house this year!' cried the swallows. 'And you'll be sure to come with us when we fly away again next time, won't you, Little-wings?'

'I will! I will!' cried the swallow, and off he went to tell the little girl that summer had come.

The Enchanted Boots

ONCE upon a time there lived in the little village of Oak Apple a very disagreeable goblin called Glum. He knew a lot of magic, and everyone was frightened of him.

Glum had a most unpleasant habit. If he were out in the hot sunshine and had forgotten his sun hat he would stop the first person he saw carrying one and make him give it up. If he happened to be out in a snowstorm without a coat he would take one from anyone he met.

No one dared say no, for they didn't know what he might do to them. But the whole village of Oak Apple was most annoyed about it, and wished that Glum would go away and never come back.

Then one day a little pixie called Tuppeny had a great idea.

'Listen!' he said to the villagers. 'Let's buy a spell to put on a pair of boots, so that whoever wears them will be walked away with, goodness knows where! We'll get Glum to put them on, and that will be the last we'll hear of him!'

'But how shall we get the spell?' asked someone. 'Glum is the only person who sells things like that.'

'I'll go and buy it from him, and pretend it is for Dame Buttercup,' said Tuppeny. 'I'll say we want to send Dame Buttercup right away, and Glum will be pleased to hear that, for he doesn't like the old dame ever since she told him he was an old rogue.'

'All right,' said the villagers. 'You go and buy the spell, Tuppeny.'

So off Tuppeny went, with a silver piece in his pocket, and knocked boldly at Glum's door.

'I want a spell to send someone goodness knows where,' he said.

'Who's it to send away?' asked Glum.

'Well, it *might* be Mother Buttercup,' answered Tuppeny slyly.

'Ha, that horrid old woman!' said Glum. 'Yes, you shall have the spell. What are you going to put it in?'

'Oh, shoes or boots, I think,' said Tuppeny.

'Well, shall I make it a kicking, leaping spell?' asked Glum. 'It would serve Mother Buttercup right if she had to go kicking and leaping, jumping and bounding all over the place. How everyone would laugh at her!'

'Yes, make it the very *worst* runaway spell you can,' said Tuppeny, grinning to himself. So Glum gave him an extra strong spell, and he ran off down the street.

'Now,' he said to the villagers, 'the next thing to do is to wait for a *very* rainy day, when Glum is out of doors. Nobody must come out of their houses except me, and I shall wear a fine pair of boots, brand new. When I meet Glum he is sure to make me take them off and give them to him, and I'll slip his spell inside them, and then we shall see some fun! How he'll wish he hadn't made it so strong.'

Three days later there came a very, very wet day. The sky was grey and the rain poured down. Glum the goblin had to go out shopping. He took his umbrella (which he had taken from Pippy the Elf in the last rain shower) and set out. His shoes were leaking and soon his feet got very wet.

'I'll look out for someone wearing really good boots,' thought Glum. But he didn't meet a single person down the street until he saw Tuppeny in the distance. Everyone was staying indoors, and was peeping through the curtains to see what would happen.

As soon as Glum met Tuppeny he stopped him and ordered him to give him his boots. Tuppeny bent down and took them off. He stuffed half the runaway spell into each and then handed them to Glum, who put them on.

And, oh, what a funny sight there was to be seen then! Those boots kicked and jumped, leapt and bounded, and took Glum's feet with them. The astonished goblin found himself dancing all over the place, and tried in vain to stop his legs from kicking in the air and jumping up and down.

'It's a spell! It's a spell!' he cried.

'Yes,' said Tuppeny, as everyone came running into the street, laughing. 'It's *your* spell, Glum – the one I bought from you on Monday. How do you like it? Ho ho ho! Ha ha ha! What a funny sight you are!'

Then Glum shook his fist at Tuppeny, but he couldn't get near him, for his feet took him off down the street. All the villagers followed, laughing in delight. This was a fine punishment for Glum!

'Where am I going? Oh, where am I going?' cried the frightened goblin, as the boots took him up the hill and down again.

'To goodness knows where!' shouted

Tuppeny. 'To goodness knows where!'

And as Glum never came back again, I think that's where he *must* have gone!

The Blowaway Morning

IT was Jimmy's birthday, and he had a lovely lot of presents. The ones he liked the best were a kite, a beautiful blue silk handkerchief and a postal order for ten pounds.

'I shall fly my kite this morning,' he said 'and wear my new handkerchief in my pocket. And I shall go to the post office to change my postal order into ten pounds and buy a new set of tools.'

First of all he took out his postal order to look at it – and, oh, dear me! the wind caught hold of it, and before Jimmy could do anything it was whirling high in the air!

'Oh, my lovely postal order!' said Jimmy, and he ran after it. But it was no use – the wind took it right out of sight, and it was lost.

Jimmy was so upset. He ran all the way home to tell his mother, and she was very sorry too.

'Oh, darling, what a pity,' she said. 'Never mind. You've still got a lot of lovely presents to play with. Take your blue silk handkerchief and go and show it to Ronnie. He will love to see it.'

So Jimmy put his handkerchief in his pocket and started off. He was really very proud of it, for it was just like Daddy's. He went to the other end of the village, where Ronnie lived, and knocked at the door.

'Ronnie's playing in the garden,' said his mother. 'You can go out to him if you like.'

So Jimmy ran into the garden, and Ronnie greeted him happily.

'Many happy returns of the day!' he said. 'Did you like the book I gave you?'

'Yes, it was great,' said Jimmy. 'Thanks very much, Ronnie. I say, look! I've brought my new handkerchief to show you. It's just like Daddy's!'

He took it from his pocket, and spread it out to show Ronnie. And, oh, my, whatever do you think? The wind swooped down and blew that away too! It tore it right out of Jimmy's hand and blew it up into the air ever so high.

'Oh, dear!' said Jimmy, almost ready to cry. 'Just look at that, Ronnie! the wind blew away my ten pound postal order this morning, and now it's taken my handkerchief. It *is* a shame!'

'Can't we go after it?' said Ronnie.

'It's gone out of sight,' said poor Jimmy. 'Oh, this is the horridest birthday that ever was! I never in my life knew such a blowaway morning!'

'Never mind,' said Ronnie. 'What other presents have you got?'

'I've got a great kite,' said Jimmy. 'If you'd like to come back with me now you can help me fly it. I thought I'd go up to Breezy Hill.'

'Oh, fine!' said Ronnie. 'Come on. Let's go now.'

So off they went to fetch the kite. Jimmy's mother was very sorry to hear about the lost handkerchief, and she gave Jimmy a chocolate cake to make up for it, and Ronnie had one too. Then Jimmy took his kite, and off they went to Breezy Hill. Up into the air soared the lovely kite, and Jimmy began to let the string out quickly, for the wind blew very strongly and the kite was pulling hard.

'Can I have a turn at holding it?' asked Ronnie, when the kite was flying high in the air.

'Yes, if you like,' said Jimmy; 'but hold tight, Ronnie – the wind's very strong.'

Ronnie took the string, and shouted joyfully to feel the kite pulling like a live thing. Then suddenly a dreadful thing happened! The wind blew so hard that it broke the string, and the kite flew higher still in the air, and then sped away over the distant woods.

'Oh!' cried Jimmy in dismay. 'There's my kite

gone now! Oh, this horrid, nasty wind! That's three things it's taken – all the presents I liked best.'

'Don't cry, Jimmy,' begged Ronnie. 'If you cry on your birthday you'll cry every day of the year, you know.'

'I'm not crying; I'm only very angry,' said Jimmy, blinking hard. 'Look, there it goes, dipping down to the ground!'

The two boys watched the kite. It dipped down in circles, and at last they could see it no longer, for it went into some trees.

'I believe if we went right over there we might find it,' said Ronnie. 'Look, Jimmy. It went over those woods, and disappeared somewhere on that little hillock of trees beyond Farmer Ricket's farm. Let's ask our mothers if we can go and look after dinner.'

Their mothers said yes, they could – so after dinner they set off. It was a long walk, but they came at last to the wood. They walked through it to Farmer Ricket's house. Then they saw the little hillock of trees in the distance. Off they went eager to see if the kite was there.

When they got there they looked all about. At first they could see nothing – then suddenly

Jimmy spied something red and yellow high up in a tree.

'There's my kite!' he shouted. 'Come on, Ronnie. Let's climb up and get it.'

Up they climbed, and soon they were busy untangling the kite from the branches. It wasn't spoilt at all, and Jimmy was very glad. Just as Ronnie was untwisting the long tail, which had got caught round a knobbly branch, he called out in surprise:

'I say, Jimmy, there's something blue caught on this branch too, as well as the tail. It doesn't belong to the kite. Look! Is it a handkerchief?'

Jimmy looked, and then he gave a cry of surprise.

'Why,' he said, 'it's the lovely blue silk handkerchief I lost this morning! The wind must have blown it right away to here! Oh, how lucky that we came to look for the kite!'

'Yes, it was the kite that found the handkerchief,' said Ronnie, with a laugh. 'What a pity the handkerchief couldn't find the postal order!'

The two boys climbed down the tree. Ronnie was just going to hand the handkerchief to Jimmy when he dropped it. In a trice the wind took it again, and off went the handkerchief into the air!

'Quick! After it!' cried Jimmy. 'We can catch it easily this time!'

The handkerchief flew into a field, and flapped about by a stream. Jimmy ran up and caught it just before it fell into the water, and then he stopped and stared hard at the stream. What was that bit of soaking wet paper there?

'Look, Ronnie!' he said. 'Can you reach down and get that bit of paper. I daren't leave go of the kite.'

Ronnie lay down by the stream, and leaned over its steep bank. He just managed to reach the soaked piece of paper. He shook the water from it, and he and Jimmy looked at it.

'*Well*,' said Jimmy, in delighted surprise, 'it's my ten pound postal order! Oh, fancy, Ronnie! It must have blown all the way here. Oh, I wonder if it matters being wet like this!'

'We'll ask your mother and see,' said Ronnie. 'Isn't it funny, Jimmy? The kite found the handkerchief and the handkerchief found the postal order! You've got all your presents back again!'

Two very happy boys ran home. Ronnie was going to have tea with Jimmy, so they went indoors together.

'Look, mother!' cried Jimmy. 'I've got my kite

and my handkerchief and my postal order! Does it matter its being wet?'

'Not a bit,' said his mother. 'We'll dry it by the fire. Then I'll give you a purse to put it in, and you and Ronnie can go and change it into money after tea. You shall wear your blue handkerchief too, and I'll pin it to your pocket; then it will be quite safe!'

'Well, it was a blowaway morning,' said Jimmy happily, 'but it was a very come-back afternoon, wasn't it, Ronnie?'

And I think it was too, don't you?

The Pixie who Paid for the Tides

THERE was once a wandering pixie who suddenly came upon the sea. He had never seen it before, and it took his breath away.

'What a lot of water all together!' he said. 'Wherever does it all come from? How lovely it is, and what a beautiful sound it makes!'

He looked and looked and looked at it. Then he made up his mind that his wandering days were over – he would build himself a little house by the sea and live there all the rest of his life.

The tide was almost full. It had about half an hour to go, but Moon-eye the pixie knew nothing about tides. He looked about for something to build his house with, and decided that he could make a lovely one with seaweed, bits of wood, and big stones.

He set to work, and in an hour's time he had a dear little house, with a door and two windows, and a chimney-pot made of an old tin. He was delighted with it.

'I'll sit at the door of my house and smoke a

pipe every morning,' he said. 'And the sea will go wisha-wisha-wisha near the door, and I shall be very happy. Now I am hungry, so I will make a fire in my little stone fireplace and cook a nice little dinner.'

He went inside and cooked a pixie dinner. Then he ate it on a table made of square rock. After that he felt sleepy, so he lay down on a bed made of silver sand and seaweed, and fell fast asleep.

Now whilst he was asleep the tide went out. It crept farther and farther down the sand, leaving bits of seaweed, old shells, wood and all kinds of odds and ends strewn about the beach.

Moon-eye woke up at last, and the first thing he did was to sit up and listen to hear the sea going wisha-wisha-wisha near the door. But it seemed as if the sound was very far away now.

He got up and went to the door. When he saw the wide beach spread out before him and the sea away down in the distance he was too surprised to say anything. Then tears came into his eyes and trickled down his cheeks.

'It's run away from me!' he said sadly. 'It didn't want me so close. And, oh! look at the nasty, dirty stretch of sand it has left near my door – all seaweed, wood, and rubbish! I shall have to clear it all up, because I hate untidy things.'

He made himself a broom and began to sweep up all the rubbish; but, dear me! there was such a lot of it that he was soon out of breath.

'I shall never finish!' he said panting. 'The sea ought to come and clear up its own mess!'

Just as he was setting to work again, up came two sly-looking pixies, with their hands in their pockets. They stared in the greatest surprise at Moon-eye, and then asked him what he was doing.

'I'm sweeping up all the rubbish that the sea has left,' he explained. 'You see, I built myself a dear little house by the water's edge, and then I went to sleep. When I woke up the sea had run away from my house, and left all this mess. I really think it should come and clear it away itself, don't you?'

The two pixies laughed loudly, but Moon-eye didn't know why. Then one looked at the other and winked.

'I'm Cric, and he's Crac,' said one of the pixies to Moon-eye. 'We've got a spell that will make the sea come and clear all this away for you if you like.'

'Oh, really?' asked Moon-eye, in surprise.

'Well, tell me how much it is and I'll buy it.'

'It costs a silver penny,' said Cric. 'I can't give you the spell, but I'll use it myself for you, and make the sea come back again.'

'All right,' said Moon-eye, handing Cric a silver penny. 'Make it come back now. It will be lovely to hear it going wisha-wisha-wisha near my door again.'

'It will only come back for a little while,' said Cric, pocketing the penny. 'It will come back slowly and eat up the rubbish for you, and go wisha-wisha-wisha near your door. Then it will run away from you again, because it doesn't like your house.'

Now it was just about the turn of the tide again, but of course Moon-eye didn't know that. He watched Cric make a big circle on the sand, and step into the middle of it. Then he and Crac joined hands and danced slowly round, singing a song that sounded like a lot of nonsense to Moon-eye – as indeed it was!

'There!' said Cric at last. 'The sea will gradually come back now. Go down to the edge of it, and see it creeping slowly up to your toes, and beyond them.'

Off went Moon-eye, wondering why Cric and Crac were laughing. He ran to the edge of the sea and stood there for a few minutes. The sea ran up to his toes, and then went back again. Next time it ran up a little bit farther. The third time it ran right round his little bare feet, so that he stood in a pool of water.

'It's all right; it's coming back again!' shouted Moon-eye to Cric and Crac. 'It's slow, but it's coming.'

Cric and Crac laughed loudly again, and went off. Moon-eye saw them go to a cottage up on the low cliff, laughing all the way. He thought they must be very good at making each other laugh.

Little by little the tide came in, and Moon-eye watched it. It took some hours to reach his little house, but he was very glad when it did, for then he could sit outside his door, smoking his pipe, and hear the water go wisha-wisha-wisha near by.

It was almost dark by this time, and Moon-eye soon went to bed. He was glad that the sea had eaten up the rubbish it had left on the beach, and he liked to know it was so near.

He woke up very late the next morning, and was delighted to see the water near his house still. He didn't know that the tide had gone out and come in again whilst he had been asleep. But he was sad to see it running away down the beach directly he sat down to smoke his pipe. He didn't know it was going out – he thought it was running away from him again.

'And look at all the rubbish on the beach again!' he thought. 'Really, the sea is very untidy. I've a good mind to ask Cric and Crac to make it come and clean it up once more. If I make it do that two or three times, perhaps it will remember.'

So he went to Cric and Crac and paid them another silver penny to make the sea come to his house again, and clear up the beach on the way.

Cric and Crac began to laugh when they saw him. Moon-eye wondered if he had got on his hat the wrong way round or something, but he was too polite to say anything.

When Cric and Crac knew what he wanted they stared at him in surprise. They hadn't thought anyone could be quite so stupid. They went indoors and talked by themselves for a minute or two, and then they came out to speak to Moon-eye.

'We are very sorry for you, because the sea keeps running away,' said Cric solemnly. 'We wish we had a spell that would make it keep near your door, but we haven't. If you'll pay us a silver penny once a week we will make the sea come up to your house once every day and once every night, and clear away any rubbish and go wisha-wisha-wisha to make you happy and peaceful. What do you say to that?'

'Well, that would be better than nothing,' said Moon-eye, thinking about it. 'I should like the beach to be well washed every day, and it would be nice to know that the sea would come to visit me regularly. I wouldn't mind it running away so much, if I knew it would have to come back again. Very well, Cric and Crac, I'll pay you a silver penny, every Monday, and you shall use your spell for me.'

So it was all arranged, and Moon-eye went back to his little house quite happy. Every Monday he took a silver penny to Cric and Crac, and every day regularly the sea swept and washed the beach for him, and came to say wisha-wisha-wisha at his door. Moon-eye was quite sure that it did all this because of the spell Cric and Crac said they were using, and he thought they were wonderful people.

But I think they are bad pixies, don't you? I'm sure they'll get into trouble when Moon-eye finds out the trick they are playing!

Pinnikin's Prank

PINNIKIN was a little brownie who used to travel about the country selling beautiful sets of dominoes. He made them himself, and then painted them very neatly with black dots, just like your dominoes at home.

He sold a great many, for they were cheap and well-made, and the pixies and elves loved a game of dominoes. Pinnikin was proud of them, and sang and whistled merrily as he went on his travels about the country.

One day he came to a fine house, and knocked at the door to see if he could sell a set of dominoes. A gnome with a long beard came to the door, and shook his head.

'No, we have plenty of dominoes,' he said. 'Not today, thank you.'

'But my dominoes are perfectly lovely,' said Pinnikin. 'Just take them to your master and ask him to have a look at them.'

'I shouldn't *dream* of bothering him,' said the gnome angrily. 'Go away!'

'But look!' said Pinnikin, pushing a box of his dominoes under the gnome's nose. 'Don't you think they are lovely?'

'No, I don't!' said the gnome crossly. 'I think they are horrid! Go away at once!'

He gave Pinnikin a push. The brownie slipped on the steps and fell. His dominoes were scattered all over the place, and he was very angry. The gnome laughed and slammed the door.

'All right! All right!' said Pinnikin, in a fine rage. 'I'll punish you, you rude old gnome!

He picked up his dominoes and went off. He made his way round to the back of the house and peeped into the garden. There he saw a great many white hens, and he smiled a naughty smile.

In a flash he was through the hedge, and one by one he caught the hens. He took his paintbrush, dipped it into his pot of black paint, and painted black spots all over each hen's suit of white feathers. How queer they looked!

'Ha, ha!' said the naughty brownie. 'You wouldn't buy my dominoes, Mr Gnome, so I've turned your fowls into domino hens. What a surprise you will get!'

Then, oh, my goodness me! a strong hand suddenly caught hold of Pinnikin, and he turned round in dismay. It was the King of Fairyland himself who had caught him!

'What is this you have done to my hens?' he said sternly.

'P-p-please, Your M-m-majesty, I didn't know they were yours!' gasped the frightened brownie.

'This is my country house, and the Queen and I are here for the weekend,' said the King sternly. 'These hens are mine. Why did you treat them like this, and paint them with all those black spots?'

'P-p-p-please, Your M-m-m-majesty, I sell dominoes that I make and paint myself,' said the brownie. 'I went to ask at the door if someone would buy a set, and the old gnome there was rude to me.'

'So you thought you would paint his hens like this!' said the King sternly. 'Well, they happen to be mine. How dare you treat the poor creatures in this way? What harm have they done to you?'

'None, Your Majesty,' said Pinnikin, beginning to cry.

'Well, you must be punished,' said the King. 'Shall I hand you over to that old gnome to be punished, or would you rather leave Fairyland altogether and do your work in the land of boys and girls?'

'I d-d-d-don't want to be punished,' said the brownie. 'I'll go right away, Your Majesty, and never get into mischief any more.'

So off he went in a great hurry, and didn't stop running until he was safely out of the gates of Fairyland.

But he soon found that nobody would buy his dominoes, for there were hundreds and hundreds of toy shops where they could be bought very cheaply. So in a short time poor Pinnikin stopped making his dominoes, and wondered what he could do.

One day he saw a little red beetle running along, and he called to him.

'Hi, red beetle, wouldn't you like me to make your coat pretty for you? Let me paint a few black spots on it and you will look very smart. All the other red beetles will envy you!'

'Very well,' said the beetle, and he let Pinnikin paint seven black spots on his bright red back. Then off he hurried, very pleased.

Soon other red beetles came to Pinnikin, and he did quite a roaring trade with them, making their plain red coats smart with five or seven black spots. Then he was happy again, and began to sing and whistle just as he had done in Fairyland.

As for the little red beetles he paints, you can see them any day. They are ladybirds, and I expect you have often wondered where they get their spots. Well, now you know!

Chipperdee and the Squirrel

ONE autumn Frisky the Squirrel collected a fine store of nuts and acorns, and hid them in all sorts of good places.

'No one will find them *here!*' he thought, as he buried some under the roots of the oak tree. 'That naughty little mouse won't think of looking under the roots, I'm sure. He found those I hid under the dead leaves, so I won't put any there this year at all.'

He tucked some acorns into a big crack in the bark of an elm tree. That was his second hiding-place. He thought it was a very good one indeed.

Then he looked about for somewhere to put an extra fine lot of beech-nuts. Whatever could he do with them?

'Aha!' said Frisky, 'I know a fine place! I'll put them in the old nest that the thrush built in the hawthorn tree! That is the best hiding-place of all!'

So he put them there. Then, as the days were getting very cold, he went to find his cosy nest.

His coat was nice and thick, but he didn't find it warm enough on frosty days. He liked to curl himself up in his nest then, and go fast asleep.

Frisky climbed into his nest, and settled down happily.

'I'll wake up some time in January, perhaps, and have a fine feast,' he said sleepily. 'Maybe a warm day will come then, and I shall be hungry. Now let me think – hazel-nuts under the oak tree roots; acorns in the elm tree; beech-nuts in – in – in –'

But Frisky was sound asleep. His soft nose was hidden in his two front paws, and he was dreaming of summer days.

Now a tiny elf had watched Frisky hiding his nuts. Her name was Chipperdee, and she was the prettiest little thing you ever saw. She had a pair of silver-tipped wings, and was dressed in a frock of spider's web. Her feet were bare, so she didn't get up very early on frosty mornings, because the cold nipped her toes.

She had made herself a bed of old brown oak leaves that still hung on the tree. She had sewed two together, and at night she slipped in between them, and was as cosy as anything. When the wind blew her bed swung here and there, and Chipperdee loved that.

It was whilst she had been swinging in her bed that she had watched Frisky hide his nuts. She thought he was a very pretty creature, and very clever at hiding all his food. She did hope that the naughty mouse wouldn't come and rob him of all his nuts, as it had done the winter before.

'I'll just watch over them for Frisky, and see that they are kept safe,' thought Chipperdee. So she did, and whenever she saw any mice about she mewed like a cat, and sent them scampering away!

Then one night there came a storm of wind and rain. The wind was so rough that it tore all the leaves off the oak tree, and Chipperdee's bed went too. It fluttered to the ground, with Chipperdee inside, and she only just slipped out before it reached the earth.

'Oh, dear!' sighed Chipperdee. 'Now what am I to do? I shall be frozen to death, for my spider's thread frock is so dreadfully thin!'

Poor Chipperdee! She simply *couldn't* find anywhere to sleep. The frost seemed to come everywhere with its cold fingers, and she would wake up shivering and trembling.

Then a day came when the sun shone warmly. The little elf sat on a branch and held her hands out to the sunshine. How she wished she could take the sun to bed with her!

Frisky the Squirrel woke up that day. He felt the sun shining into his cosy nest, and he stretched himself.

'I'm hungry!' he said. 'Oh, I *am* hungry! I must really go out and get some nuts! I hid such a lovely lot. I will have a fine meal, and then I'll come and curl up in my nest again, for I'm sure it will be bitterly cold when the sun has gone.'

So he popped out of his nest and looked around.

'Now where did I put those nuts and acorns?' he wondered. 'I must think.'

He thought and thought – but it was no use; he couldn't remember where he had put them. Then he ran here and there looking for them, but still he couldn't find them. It was such a pity, for he really was dreadfully hungry.

Then Chipperdee suddenly saw him.

'Why, here's the squirrel wakened up for a feast!' she thought. 'I wonder if he'll be pleased when he sees all his nuts are safe.'

She watched him for a little while, wondering why he didn't get his acorns and nuts. Then she saw him sit and frown very hard indeed.

'Why, the pretty little creature has forgotten

where he hid them!' she said. 'I must tell him.'

She spread her wings and flew to where Frisky was sitting on a branch.

'*I* know where your nuts are!' she said. 'Shall I show you? I frightened all the mice away when they came sniffing by, so they are quite safe.'

She flew to the roots of the oak tree, and Frisky gladly dug up his hazel-nuts. Then she flew to the crack in the bark of the elm tree, and the delighted squirrel took out his acorns. Last of all the elf showed him the thrush's nest, and there, quite safe, were all his beech-nuts. He *was* so pleased.

He made a good meal, and Chipperdee accepted the very best hazel-nut. She nibbled at it, and enjoyed it very much. Then as the sun went down she began to shiver.

'I must go,' she said. 'So must you, Frisky, or the frost will get you. Put the rest of your nuts into the thrush's nest, for they will be quite safe there – and don't forget where they are next time!'

'No, I won't,' said Frisky. 'It was so kind of you to come and tell me. I do wish I could do something for you in return. Is there anything I can do, Chipperdee?'

'No, nothing,' said the elf. 'I should be quite

happy if only I could find a nice bed to sleep in. But the frost comes everywhere I go, and makes me so miserable.'

'You poor little thing!' cried Frisky. 'Why, I know what I can do! I'll take you back with me to share my nest! You shall cuddle up with me there, and I'm sure you'll be as warm as can be. Do come, Chipperdee. Then, when I wake up again, you can remember where I put my nuts, so you will be very useful to me indeed,'

So off Chipperdee went with Frisky, and for the first time for many nights she was as warm as toast. She cuddled into the squirrel's soft fur, and slept like a top. Frisky slept all the next day and the next and the next without waking. So every morning Chipperdee slipped out quietly to visit her friends, and every night she slipped back again into the warmth.

And when Frisky woke up and wanted his nuts again she told him where to find them, for of course he had forgotten! When springtime came they both went off to play together in the trees, and you couldn't have found a happier pair anywhere!

Tiddler Mouse Talks

TIDDLER MOUSE was very fond of talking. He talked all day long, and all night long too, to anyone that would listen to him, and sometimes he poked his head out of his mouse-hole and talked cheekily to the cat, who sharpened his claws and said nothing.

One day the mice held a meeting about the cat.

'She has eaten six of us this week,' said Whisker Mouse.

'She ate five last week,' said Tailer Mouse.

'She will eat seven next week – unless we do something to stop her,' said Nibbler Mouse.

Then Tiddler Mouse got up and began to talk. How he talked! On and on he went without stopping, full of ideas of how to stop the cat from catching and killing them.

'Let *us* talk for a moment,' said Nibbler Mouse, at last. 'Now one of your ideas, Tiddler, is a good one – and that is, to put gloves on the cat's feet so that she cannot use her claws to catch us with.'

'Yes!' said Tiddler, delighted that he had been listened to. 'Yes! Now that is really a fine idea – yes, it is! If only we do that we shall never need to fear the cat again!'

'Well, Tiddler, it really is the best thing you have said,' said Whisker Mouse. 'Now, when would you like to put the gloves on the cat? To-morrow? I'll get my wife to make them tonight, if you like.'

Tiddler Mouse turned pale. He hadn't for a moment thought that *he* would have to carry out his idea.

'Oh,' he said, 'I am only a small mouse. You are much bigger and cleverer than I am. *You* ought to have the honour of putting the gloves on the cat, Whisker Mouse – or you, Nibbler Mouse, – or you, Tailer.'

'Not at all,' said Tailer firmly. 'It was your idea, and you spoke about it for quite an hour. You shall put the gloves on the cat. Are you afraid?'

'Certainly not,' said Tiddler, although his tail was trembling with fright. 'I'll do it!'

'Then my wife shall make the gloves tonight,' said Whisker. So Mrs Whisker Mouse made them, and the next day another meeting was held, and the gloves were given to Tiddler.

'They ought to be *tied* on,' said Tiddler. 'I haven't any ribbon.'

'I know where there is some string!' said Tailer Mouse, and off he went to fetch it. He was soon back with a long piece, which he bit into four, one for each glove.

'Thank you,' said poor Tiddler.

'Now are you ready?' asked Whisker Mouse, peeping out of the mouse-hole into the kitchen. 'The cat is sitting washing itself in front of the fire. You could easily slip out now and put the gloves on its paws, Tiddler.'

'Very well,' said Tiddler boldly, and he went to the mouse-hole. Then he looked back.

'I shall have to ask one of you to come with me to hold the cat, whilst I put the gloves on,' he said. 'I am not strong enough to do both things at once.'

Nobody said a word. They just stared at Tiddler.

'Well!' said Tiddler. 'Who's coming? Will you, Tailer?'

'I don't think so,' said Tailer. 'I've some work to do.'

'Will you, Whisker – or you, Nibbler?' asked Tiddler. But neither of them would hold the cat for Tiddler.

'Well!' said Tiddler, pretending to be very much surprised. 'You *are* a lot of cowards! You are all bigger than I am and yet you won't come out and help me glove the cat! If I am brave enough to put gloves on her paws, I should have thought that one of you big mice was brave enough to hold her for me.'

Nobody spoke at all. The cat in the kitchen stretched herself and purred.

'I must go to my work,' said Tailer, and he ran off.

'I have some nibbling to do,' said Whisker, and he vanished. Soon there was no one there but Tiddler, and he began to laugh.

'Ha ha!' he cried. 'Ha ha! What a joke! I shan't put gloves on the cat, not I! She can put them on herself if she wants to!'

He threw them out of the mouse-hole into the kitchen, and then scampered off, talking at the top of his voice.

'How brave I am! Oh, how wonderful I am! I nearly put gloves on the cat!'

Buttercup Magic

CHIPPY was a gnome who helped old Mother Grumps with her farm-work. He ran here and there for her, milked the cows, made the butter, and groomed the horses. He was a very hard-working gnome, and Mother Grumps had no fault to find with him.

But she could not for the life of her think where all her butter went to. Such a lot was made, and put aside to sell, and yet when the time came to sell it there never seemed to be the right amount.

'Where can it go to?' asked Mother Grumps. 'Do *you* take any, husband?'

'Not I,' said her husband. 'I don't like butter enough to take any, as you know.'

'Well, do you take any?' she asked her son. But he laughed and shook his head.

'Why, mother, I would never take butter at all if you didn't make me,' he said. 'Nasty, greasy stuff!'

Then Mother Grumps went to Sally Lingum-bob, her old, old nanny, and shouted in her ear:

'Do you touch any of the butter set out in the dairy, Sally?'

But Sally shook her head from side to side indignantly.

'Don't I sit up here in my room all day long?' she asked. 'How could my poor old legs take me down to the dairy and back again without you helping me?'

Well, Mother Grumps knew that was true, and she was more puzzled than ever. She really didn't know what to think.

'You ask that little gnome,' said old Sally, who had never liked Chippy. 'I expect *he* could tell you where it goes to!'

'Dear me, I'd forgotten Chippy,' said Mother Grumps. 'But I don't think it *can* be the gnome, Sally, for he never takes butter at any meal, you know. He even has his bread dry.'

'Well, you ask him, that's all,' said Sally.

So Mother Grumps asked him.

'I can't think what happens to the butter, Chippy,' she said. 'Do you ever go into the dairy and take any?'

'Never, madam,' said Chippy. 'I don't like butter at all. Why, as you know, I never have it on my bread when I sit in the kitchen at tea with you every day.'

'No, you don't. That's quite true,' said Mother Grumps. 'Well, well, well! This is a most extraordinary thing. Here's a household that doesn't like butter, and yet it disappears steadily.'

The butter still went on vanishing, and at last Mother Grumps went to see an old friend of hers, a wise woman who lived on Blowaway Hill. She told her about her puzzle, and the wise woman laughed.

'Why, my dear,' she said, 'I will soon find out for you. I'll come along tomorrow and solve the mystery.'

So the next day she came trotting along over the buttercup fields, her skirts all yellow with pollen. Before she reached Mother Grumps's farm, she stooped and picked a fine large buttercup.

With this in her hand she knocked at Mother Grumps's door.

'Come in, come in,' cried Mother Grumps, opening the door wide. 'I'm so pleased to see you. What have you brought that buttercup for, my dear?'

'Let me hold it under your chin for a moment,' said the wise woman. Mother Grumps held up her chin, and the old woman held the buttercup underneath.

'Now it's your turn,' she said to Farmer Grumps, and she held it under *his* chin.

Then the son had to have it held under his chin too, and he said the buttercup tickled him dreadfully.

'Nonsense!' laughed the wise woman. 'Now where's old Sally Lingumbob, my dear?'

'Upstairs,' said Mother Grumps, and up they went to Sally's room. She had to have the buttercup held under *her* chin too, and she grumbled about it, and said it made her neck ache to hold her head up like that, all for a whim of the wise woman's. Why couldn't she use her buttercups on her own folk, instead of coming worrying Mother Grumps's family?

The wise woman laughed, and made no answer. 'Is there any one else in your house?' she asked.

'Yes,' said Mother Grumps, 'there's Chippy the gnome.'

'I'll try him too with my buttercup,' said the wise woman, and she went to where the gnome was sweeping out the scullery.

He lifted up his head in surprise when she told him to, and she held the golden buttercup underneath his chin. Then she thanked him and went into the living room with Mother Grumps and shut the door.

'Chippy takes your butter,' she said gravely. 'He is very, very, very fond of it.'

'Oh, nonsense!' said Mother Grumps. 'Why, he won't even have it on his bread at tea-time.'

'That's only to make you think he doesn't like it,' said the wise woman. 'I expect he goes straight home afterwards and eats a whole lot. I tell you he loves it. Watch your dairy tonight and see if anyone gets into it.'

So that night Father Grumps watched his dairy, for there was a great deal of butter there, all waiting to go to market to be sold. And sure enough, at midnight, when everything was dark and silent, the dairy window slid up and someone slipped in, and ran softly over to the pile of butter.

'Hoy!' shouted Farmer Grumps, and jumped up from the chair in which he had been sitting half asleep. 'I've got you!'

He caught hold of someone's shoulder, and called loudly for his son to come and light a candle. Mother Grumps and her son came running along in their dressing-gowns, and soon a candle was lighted, and everyone looked to see who the thief was.

And it was Chippy, the gnome who vowed he never took butter, because he couldn't bear it! There he stood, trembling, his hands smeared with butter, and a large slice of bread spread with butter a centimetre thick!

'Oho!' cried Mother Grumps angrily. 'So it's you, is it, Chippy, you naughty little gnome! Well, you shall just have to go away and never come back again.'

Then Chippy went down on his knees and begged for forgiveness.

'I'll always be good now,' he wept. 'Please take me back, master and mistress. I'll never take butter again. But, oh, how did you find out it was I who took it?'

'How *did* the wise woman find out?' asked Farmer Grumps.

Mother Grumps shook her head. She hadn't thought to ask. But she made up her mind to find out the next day.

She went to Blowaway Hill and told the wise woman what had happened. 'But, my dear, how did you find out it was Chippy?' she asked.

'Oh, that's easy!' said the wise woman. 'Didn't you know that buttercups once had a butter spell put on them? Whenever you hold them under anyone's chin, you can find out if that person likes butter, for you will see a golden light come under their chin, just the colour of new-made butter. As soon as I popped the buttercup under Chippy's chin I knew he was the thief, for the golden light almost dazzled me! So I knew he was very, very fond of butter!'

'Well, you were quite right,' said Mother Grumps. 'But, dear me, fancy buttercups being magic enough to tell you all that! I must really tell my friends!'

'No, don't do that,' said the wise woman. 'I want it to be kept secret.'

But Mother Grumps simply *couldn't* keep a secret, and soon all her village knew about the buttercups. Then the next village got to know, and the next, and the next. And now there isn't a place in the kingdom that doesn't know that buttercups will tell you if you like butter.

You know it, of course, don't you? – but if you don't, be sure to pick a fine large buttercup this June and hold it under your sister's chin, or your brother's. Say, 'Do you like butter?' and you will see the answer underneath your brother's chin, as clear as can be – for a lovely golden light will shine there, as yellow as new-made butter!

The Magician's Inkpot

THE famous magician Dear-me lived in Crinkle Cottage with his little cook Ooh-my. She was the only servant that Dear-me had, except for a slave that came whenever he rubbed a magic ring he wore on his finger.

This slave would do anything the magician commanded. He would bring food, drink, dresses, gold, jewels – anything. Ooh-my's eyes nearly dropped out of her head when she saw what the slave could do. She wished she could have a slave of the ring too but no matter how much she rubbed her own little brass ring no slave appeared to do her bidding.

Now, one day the magician packed up his bag and went away for a week-end, for he was rather tired. He left Ooh-my in charge of Crinkle Cottage, and told her to be sure and keep everything nice and clean. Then he said good-bye and went off to catch the bus.

Now the next morning, when Ooh-my was

sweeping the floor, what should she find but a ring – and it was the very ring that the magician used to rub to make the slave come to do his bidding.

'Ooh my!' said Ooh-my. 'He must have dropped it without knowing! Ooh, it's the first time I've ever held it in my hands!'

She slipped it on her little finger, and then an idea came into her silly head. Why shouldn't she call up the slave herself, and set him to do some task? How grand it would be to feel as powerful as that!

Without stopping to think, she began to rub the ring with her duster. At once there was a loud crash, smoke filled the room, and there before her was the slave of the ring. But when he saw that it was not the magician who had called him, he did not bow low, as he usually did, but frowned deeply.

Ooh-my was frightened. She wished she hadn't used the ring. She didn't know what to say to the slave at all. So all she said was 'Ooh my! Ooh!'

'Tell me something to do!' commanded the slave in a booming voice. 'Quick! Tell me something to do, or I shall disappear and take you with me.'

'Ooh my!' groaned the little cook. 'What shall I tell him?'

'Quick!' commanded the slave impatiently. 'Set me a task.'

Ooh-my suddenly saw that the magician's inkpot was almost empty.

'Fill the inkpot with ink!' she said.

At once the slave took a large bottle from the air and began to fill the pot with ink. Ooh-my ran thankfully from the room. She couldn't bear to be with the slave any longer. She went to the kitchen and made herself a cup of hot, strong tea, for she was really feeling very upset.

She hadn't sat there more than twenty minutes when she began to wonder what the slave was doing. He must have filled the inkpot a long time ago. Perhaps he had done that and gone. Ooh-my hoped very much he had.

She made up her mind to go and see. So she left the kitchen and tiptoed to the parlour door; and, oh, dear me! whatever should she see but the slave *still* pouring ink into the inkpot! Of course, it was quite full, running over. The ink had overflowed on to the new table-cloth and run to the floor. All the pretty carpet was soaked in ink, and a big stream of black was slowly making its way to the door where Ooh-my stood.

'Ooh my!' said the little cook, in horror. 'Ooh my! Whatever will the magician say? Just look at all that ink! Stop, slave, stop!'

But the slave took no notice of Ooh-my at all. He simply went on pouring out the ink from the endless bottle, and the black stream got bigger and bigger, till it swirled round Ooh-my's feet and made her brown shoes black.

She gave a shriek of dismay and tore back to the kitchen. But the ink followed her there, and soon her nice clean kitchen was all black and wet with ink.

'What shall I do? What shall I do?' wept Ooh-my. 'This is terrible! How can I get that slave away? He won't take any notice of what I tell him!'

The ink rose higher and higher, and at last Ooh-my opened the back door and went out, for she felt certain she would be drowned in ink if she didn't. The ink ran out down the path, and the passing gnomes and brownies stared in amazement.

And who should Ooh-my see coming down the road but the magician Dear-me himself! He had got tired of his holiday and had come back sooner than he had expected.

How glad Ooh-my was to see him! She ran up to him in a great hurry.

'Master! master!' she cried. 'Come quickly! That slave of yours is filling the kitchen with ink, and I can't make him stop!'

The magician ran to his cottage. His feet squelched in the ink, and he was splashed with black from head to foot. When the slave saw him he stopped pouring out the ink and bowed very low.

The magician clapped his hands twice.

'Go!' he said. 'Vanish! Disappear! You are in disgrace!'

The slave vanished with a bang, and the room was filled with smoke again. Ooh-my waded in behind her master, crying bitterly as she saw all the damage that had been done.

'Where is my ring?' asked the magician. 'Give it to me. And remember this, Ooh-my – never meddle with my things again. I shall not punish you, because the mess you will have to clear up is punishment enough. Stop crying, and go and get pails of water.'

Ooh-my handed her master the ring, and wiped her eyes. She went to get water from the pump, and all that day and the next she spent trying to get rid of the ink.

'I'll never – *never* – NEVER meddle with things that don't concern me again!' she vowed,

as she scrubbed away at the black ink-marks.
And, so the magician tells me, she never has!

The Pig with a Straight Tail

THERE was once a pig whose tail was as straight as a poker. This worried him very much, because all the tails belonging to his brothers and sisters were very curly indeed.

'Ha!' said his little fat sisters. 'Look at Grunts! Whoever saw a pig with a straight tail before?'

'Ho!' said his brothers. 'Look at Grunts! Whoever saw a pig without a kink in his tail before?'

Poor Grunts was very much upset about it.

'I really must get my tail curly somehow,' he thought to himself. 'Now what can I do?'

He thought a little while and then he trotted off to old Dame Criss-cross.

'Sometimes her hair is quite straight and sometimes it is curly,' he said to himself. 'I wonder what she does to it. I will ask her.'

So he knocked on her little front door with his hoof. Dame Criss-cross opened it, and was most surprised to see Grunts there.

'What do you want?' she asked.

'I want to know how to curl my tail,' said Grunts. 'I know you curl your hair, so I thought perhaps you could tell me.'

Dame Criss-cross laughed till the tears came into her eyes. Then she went into her bedroom and fetched a great big curling-pin, the biggest she had got.

'Here you are, Grunts,' she said. 'Let me put your tail into this curling-pin and it will curl beautifully.'

She rolled Grunts' tail up in the pin, and, oh dear! it did hurt! Grunts groaned loudly, but he so badly wanted a curly tail that he put up with the pain like a hero.

Off he went back to the pigsty, and, dear me! how all the big pigs and little pigs roared with laughter to see Grunts with his tail done up in a large curling-pin.

Next morning Grunts ran off to Dame Criss-cross again, and she undid it for him. Oh, what a fine curly tail he had! It twisted itself up like a spring, and Grunts was terribly proud of it. He stood with his back to all the other pigs whenever he could, and they admired his tail very much, for it was even curlier than theirs.

But then a dreadful thing happened. It began to rain. Grunts took no notice, for he didn't mind

the rain at all; but his beautiful curly tail got wet
and all the curl came out!

'Your tail's straight! Your tail's straight!' cried
all the pigs, crowding round him. Grunts looked
over his back, and, sure enough, his tail was as
straight as a poker again.

'Oh, bother!' said Grunts, in dismay. 'It's no
good putting it into curlers, that's quite plain.
Now what shall I do?'

'Go to Tips the pixie and get her to put a curly
spell in your tail,' said the biggest pig of all.

So off went Grunts to Tips' little cottage and
banged at her door with his hoof.

'What do you want, Grunts?' she asked.

'Can you put a curly spell in my tail?' asked
Grunts. 'It's so dreadfully straight.'

'Well, I'll try,' said Tips, doubtfully. 'But I
don't know if I've a spell that is strong enough.
Your tail is really too *terribly* straight!'

She fetched a blue bowl, and put into it six
strange things – a golden feather with a blue tip, a
spider's web heavy with dew, a centre of a young
daisy, the whisker of a gooseberry, a hair from a
red squirrel, and a spoonful of moonlight taken
from a puddle. Then she stirred the mixture up
together, singing a little magic song.

'Now turn round and put your tail in the

bowl,' said Tips. 'The spell will make it curly.'

So Grunts turned round and put his straight little tail into the blue bowl. The pixie stirred the mixture all over it, and gradually it became curlier and curlier. Tips was delighted.

'It has made it curly,' she said. 'But I don't know how long it will stay like that, Grunts.'

'Will rain hurt it?' asked the little pig.

'No,' said Tips. 'I don't think so. My, you do look fine!'

Off went Grunts back to the pigsty, and all the pigs admired him very much. But – wasn't it a pity? – the sun came out and shone down so hotly that poor Grunts' tail began to go limp again! And soon it was just as straight as ever. The sun had melted away the curly spell.

'Well, I'm sure I don't know *what* to do!' said Grunts in dismay.

'What's the matter?' asked an old witch, who happened to be passing by. So Grunts told her his trouble.

'Oh, you want a very, very strong spell,' said the witch. 'You had better come to me – I can give you one that will make your tail very curly indeed.'

Now, the wicked old witch didn't mean to do anything of the sort. She just wanted to get hold of Grunts and make him into bacon, for he was a very fat little pig. But Grunts didn't know she was wicked, and he felt most excited.

'Come to me at midnight tonight,' said the witch. 'My cottage is in the middle of Hawthorn Wood.'

So that night, just about half-past eleven, Grunts set out. It was very dark, and when he got into the wood it was darker still. Grunts began to feel frightened.

Then something made him jump terribly.

'Too-whit, too-whit!' said a loud voice.

'Too-whoo, too-whoo!' said another. Grunts gave a squeal and began to run.

He didn't know it was only a pair of owls calling to one another. Then something else gave him a fright. The moon rose and looked at him through the trees.

'Ooh!' squealed the little pig. 'What is it? It's a giant's face looking at me!'

He stumbled on through the wood, quite losing his way. Suddenly he heard two voices nearby, and against the light of the moon he saw two witches.

'Have you seen a little fat pig?' asked one.

'No,' said the other. 'Why?'

'Oh, one was coming to me to get his tail made

curly!' said the first one, with a laugh. 'Silly little pig! He didn't know I was going to catch him and make him into bacon!'

Grunts crouched down in the bushes, and stayed quite still until the witches had gone away. All his bristles stood up on his back with fright, his tail curled up with fear, and he shivered like a jelly.

'What an escape I've had!' he thought. 'Ooh, that wicked old witch. I'll go straight home as soon as it's dawn.'

So when day came he looked around him, found the right path, and scampered home as fast as ever he could. *Wasn't* he glad to see the pigsty. But what a surprise he had when he got there!

'Oh, your tail *is* lovely and curly!' cried all his brothers and sisters. 'Did the old witch put a spell on it?'

'No,' said Grunts, in surprise, looking at his curly tail in delight. 'Now whatever made it go like that? Why, I was almost frightened out of my life!'

'It was the fright that made your tail curl!' said an old pig, wisely. 'That's what it was! Didn't you feel something funny about it last night?'

'Now I come to think of it, I did,' said the little pig. 'Oh, my, what a funny thing! I escaped the old witch, got a terrible fright, and a curly tail! I wonder if it will last.'

Day after day Grunts looked at his tail – and so far it is still as curly as ever. He *is* so pleased about it!

Wizard Grumpity-Groo

THERE was a most unpleasant wizard called Grumpity-Groo. He settled down in the very middle of Fairyland, and nobody could get rid of him. Even the Fairy Queen herself could do nothing, and when she called one morning at the wizard's little cottage he was very rude to her.

'Good morning, madam, and goodbye,' he said, opening and shutting the door all in one movement. And that was all he said. Wasn't he rude?

Kimmy the elf was with the Queen, and he was very cross that anyone should be so rude to her. So he quite lost his temper, and threw open one of the wizard's windows and gave him a good smack.

The wizard was angry. He pulled the elf into his cottage, shut the window with a bang, and then turned to Kimmy with a deep frown.

'You shall be taught a lesson,' he said. 'You shall be my servant for a year and a day.'

Poor Kimmy! He did have to work hard. He

had to do all the work of the cottage, draw all the magic circles that the wizard wanted – and he needed a good many – stir the magic cauldron over the fire, and collect the herbs that Grumpity-Groo commanded him to find.

But all the time he was wondering how to defeat the wizard, who was really a very unpleasant fellow. He was much worse than the Queen had guessed, and Kimmy was horrified at the things he did.

Then one day Grumpity-Groo began boasting that he was very clever.

'Oh, I'm the greatest wizard in the whole world!' he said. 'No one in Fairyland is so powerful as I! One day I will catch the Fairy Queen and marry her. Then I shall be King of Fairyland, and do just what I like! I shall shut the fairies up into jars, and throw them to the bottom of the sea!'

'Oooh!' said Kimmy, very much afraid. 'But are you more powerful than the old witch Gloomy, who lives right at the other end of Fairyland?'

'Pooh!' said the wizard. 'Of course.'

'But she can do *wonderful* things!' said the elf. 'She can turn herself into a black cat whenever she likes!'

'So can I!' cried the wizard, and in a twinkling he vanished, and in his place was the largest black cat that Kimmy had ever seen. It came towards the elf, hissing and showing its large claws. Kimmy was frightened and ran into a corner. Then the cat laughed and in another moment it changed back to the wizard.

Then a wonderful idea came to the elf. He pretended to be scornful.

'That's nothing,' he said. 'Any old wizard could do that! Could you change yourself into a beetle with green spots and yellow stripes?'

'Easy!' cried the wizard, and in a flash he had disappeared, and in his place was a large beetle with green spots and yellow stripes, running across the floor.

Then it vanished and the wizard again appeared.

'Would you like me to do anything else to show my wonderful powers?' he asked.

'Yes,' said Kimmy boldly. 'Change yourself into a kilo of sugar, and put yourself into that bag over there! I don't believe that any wizard could do a thing like that!'

Grumpity-Groo laughed loudly.

'You do give me easy things to do!' he said. 'Why, even a very young wizard could do that!

Ask me something harder!'

'Ah, you only say that because you can't do it!' cried Kimmy.

The wizard frowned.

'You are bold to speak to me like this!' he growled. 'I will do as you say, and then when I change back to my own form, I shall punish you for being so rude to me.'

He vanished. The elf waited to see what would happen. On the floor appeared a heap of lump sugar, and then lump by lump it jumped into the bag on the table. When the last lump had gone inside, the elf rushed to the bag. He took a piece of string and tied it tightly round the neck – the wizard was a prisoner.

Kimmy rushed out of the cottage, and ran as hard as he could to the Fairy Queen's palace. The lumps of sugar jumped about like mad, but they couldn't get out and change back to the wizard because the elf had tied up the bag so tightly.

At last he arrived panting at the palace gate. He ran up the steps and begged to see the Queen. In two minutes he was before her, and she was asking him what was the matter.

'I've got the wizard in this bag!' said Kimmy. 'What shall we do with him? He has changed himself into lumps of sugar.'

'But whatever made him do that?' asked the Queen in astonishment. Quickly Kimmy told her all that had happened, and she was very glad when she heard how he had defeated the wicked wizard.

'But what shall we *do* with him now that we've got him?' asked Kimmy. 'We must think of something quickly, because I expect the sugar will make a hole in the bag by the way it is jumping about, and then, oh, dear me! he will change back to his old shape and punish us all most severely.'

The Queen thought hard for a moment, then she called to an attendant.

'Bring a bowl of hot water!' she commanded. The attendant brought it and put it on a table by the Queen. Then with trembling hands Her Majesty opened the bag, turned it upside down, and emptied all the sugar lumps into the water!

They made a curious sizzling sound and the water turned bright green.

'All the sugar will melt, and that will be the end of the wizard!' said the Queen to the astonished elf. They watched the water. The lumps gradually fell to pieces, and soon there was nothing to be seen but the green water. Then it suddenly turned back to its right colour again, and the Queen gave a sigh of relief.

'That's the end of him!' she said. 'What a dreadful person he was! And how clever of you to think of such a good idea, Kimmy! I will give you ten bags of gold and a castle of your own. Then you will be rich for the rest of your life!'

She kept her word, and Kimmy became a very grand person indeed. He married and took his wife with him to his castle, and there they live happily to this very day!

Angelina's Great Adventure

ANGELINA was the prettiest doll that was ever seen in any nursery. Her hair was in golden curls, her eyes were bright blue, with curling lashes, and she could walk and talk.

She was the queen of Jean's toy cupboard, and all the other toys were fond of her, especially the ugly old rag doll. But she wouldn't even *look* at him!

'Go away!' she said to the faithful rag doll. 'I don't like your horrid face. Go and wash it.'

But however much the poor rag doll washed it, the grey wouldn't come off, and he was very unhappy.

One day a dreadful thing happened. A gnome looked in at the nursery window and saw Angelina sitting in her little chair, looking simply beautiful.

'You shall marry me!' he cried, and he jumped in through the window, caught her up, and ran off with her.

'Help! Help!' screamed Angelina in a terrible

fright. All the toys looked out of the cupboard, and when the rag doll saw what was happening he tore after the gnome.

But outside was a little motor car, and the gnome stuffed Angelina into the front seat, sat beside her, took the steering wheel and drove off!

The rag doll didn't know *what* to do!

'Oh, where has he taken her?' he cried in despair.

'I should think he's taken her to Toy-town,' said a pixie nearby. 'He can't marry her anywhere except in Toy-town because she's a toy.'

The rag doll rushed back to the nursery and jumped into a clockwork motor car. The Teddy bear wound it up for him, and off he went after the gnome. He tore along the road to Toy-town at a tremendous speed, frightening the elves and pixies almost out of their lives.

'Toot-toot-! Toot-toot!' went his horn, and everyone sprang out of the way.

At last he arrived at Toy-town, and he asked some wooden soldiers if they had seen anything of a gnome with a lovely doll beside him.

'Oh, yes,' said the soldiers, pointing. 'He has taken her to his house. There it is over in that corner. She was crying when she went in.'

The rag doll drove up to the house, which was very like the doll's house in the nursery. He jumped from his car and looked up at the windows. In one of the top ones he saw Angelina, looking down at him with tears in her eyes.

'Save me! Save me!' she cried. 'The gnome has gone to see about our wedding!'

The rag doll looked round wildly. Opposite the house was a fire station, and in a flash he ran across to it. He drove out the fire engine, wound the ladder up to the high window, and ran lightly up it. He threw open the window and helped Angelina out. Down the ladder they went, and arrived safely on the ground.

'Hurrah!' said the rag doll. 'I'll just put the fire engine back, and then we'll drive home in the car.'

He drove the fire engine into its place again, and then ran to the car. He bent down to wind it up – but, oh, goodness me! whatever do you think? In his wild journey to Toy-town the rag doll had bumped over many a rough road, and the key that wound up the clockwork motor had dropped out! It was nowhere to be seen!

The rag doll stood up in dismay, and at that very moment who should come down the street but the gnome himself! He gave an angry shout and raced towards Angelina and the rag doll.

'Come on,' said the rag doll, and he took hold of Angelina's hand and pulled her down the road. 'We must run!'

Off they ran, panting and puffing, for all they were worth; but the gnome panted the most, for he was fat. Soon they had left him behind, but the rag doll was worried, for he did not know how they were going to get away from Toy-town, and he was afraid that sooner or later the gnome would catch them.

On they ran, and on and on. Soon they came to the market of Toy-town, and the rag doll stopped and looked round. What a lot of things were sold there – honey in jars, big coloured balloons, paper windmills, little sunshades, furniture for a doll's house, and hundreds of other things.

The rag doll put his hand into his pocket and took out some money. He went over to the stall that sold balloons and sunshades.

'Eight balloons and two sunshades,' he said, and put down the money for them. As soon as he had got them he took hold of Angelina's hand and ran with her to a grassy hill not far away. The wind was blowing very strongly there, and Angelina's hair flew out behind her.

The rag doll undid the string round the balloons, and began to blow them up much bigger. Soon all eight were bigger than he was, and the wind blew them very strongly.

'Take one of these sunshades, but don't open it till I tell you,' said the rag doll. 'Now, let me tie this string round you. The balloons will carry us away next time the wind blows.'

'Oh, there's the gnome! Look!' cried Angelina in a fright and pointed down the hill. Sure enough the gnome was tearing up the hill; but when he saw what they were doing he tore back to the market and bought six balloons for himself. Then off he ran again to the windy hill.

The rag doll hurriedly tied himself and Angelina to the balloons, and when the next gust of wind came they jumped into the air and found themselves carried gently along by the eight balloons. The gnome also jumped into the air with his and the wind blew him along after them.

'Whatever shall we do?' cried Angelina, the tears pouring down her pretty face. 'Oh, do save me.'

Nearer and nearer came the gnome, for he was lighter than the rag doll and the doll, and the wind blew him along more quickly. When he was almost up to them the rag doll took a pin from his coat and one by one he burst the eight balloons above him, crying out as he did so, 'Open your sunshade, Angelina!'

She opened it, and as the last balloon burst, she dropped downwards, her open sunshade held above her like a little parachute. The rag doll did the same, and the gnome shook his fist at them in rage, for he had not thought of buying a sunshade.

At last the rag doll and Angelina reached the ground in safety, and, wonder of wonders, they landed at the bottom of their own garden. It took them just two minutes to run up the path, climb in at the nursery window, and shout 'Hurrah!'

What a rejoicing there was! The toys all gave a tea-party in honour of the brave rag doll and at the end Angelina kissed him and said that he was the very best friend she had ever had.

How delighted he was! His grey face blushed bright red, and he beamed with joy.

'I am very happy,' he said, 'and there's just one thing that would make me happier still! I *would* like to know what happened to that gnome!'

'I can tell you!' said a sparrow, looking in at the window. 'All his balloons went flat, one by one, and he fell into a duck pond! Ha ha! How the ducks pecked at him!'

'Serve him right!' cried everyone. And so it did!

One Good Turn Deserves Another

IN the garden belonging to Billy and Jane there were a great many hazelnut trees. Billy was always pleased when the autumn came, because then he and Jane took their little baskets and went to pick the nuts. There were hundreds of them, and it didn't take them very long to fill their baskets.

One year, when October came, little red squirrels scampered into the garden. They went to the hazel trees and began to strip the nuts from them, gnawing holes in them with their sharp teeth and then taking out the sweet nut inside.

'Oh, Mummy, look!' cried Jane in dismay. 'The squirrels are stealing our nuts. There will be none left for us!'

'Shall we go and shoo them away?' asked Billy.

'I think there will be lots left for you,' said Mummy, smiling. 'They are such pretty little creatures. Surely you can spare a few nuts for them?'

'Of course we can!' said Jane. 'If they are hungry, let them have them!'

So they did not chase away the squirrels, but let them sit in the trees and eat the nuts.

'Look, Jane!' said Billy one morning. 'That little fellow isn't eating his nuts. He's carrying them away somewhere! I wonder why.'

'Perhaps he's going to store them up for the winter,' said Jane, wisely.

'But squirrels sleep all winter,' said Billy.

'Mummy said they wake up when it's warm and sunny,' said Jane. 'They come out from their hidey-holes then, and I expect they feel hungry. Perhaps they eat the nuts they have stored.'

Billy and Jane filled their baskets many times with nuts. There were plenty for them and plenty for the red squirrels too. The squirrels got quite used to the children and sat up in the hazel trees peering down at them whilst they picked the big clusters of nuts.

Soon the leaves fell from the nut trees, and winter set in. It was cold and dark, and often fogs came so that Billy and Jane could not go out. They moped indoors, longing for the sun to shine again.

Then one day in January the sun did shine. How it shone! The sky was purest blue without a

single cloud, and the white snow that lay on the
ground glittered and shone.

'Mummy, do let Billy and me go for a lovely
long walk,' begged Jane. 'It's a glorious day and
we could go to Windy Woods all by ourselves,
and take our lunch with us.'

'Very well,' said Mummy. 'I'll make you some
sandwiches, and you shall have some cakes, two
apples and some hot milk in the thermos flask.'

She packed them all these things, and they set
off happily over the snow. Billy carried the
basket, and Jane led the way.

When they had got halfway to the woods they
sat down for a rest and ate their apples. Then
Jane saw some queer footmarks in the snow and
got up to see what they were.

'They are the footmarks of a stoat!' said Billy.
'Let's follow them and see where they lead.'

They led right up to Windy Woods, and then
disappeared. Billy and Jane walked into the heart
of the wood, and then discovered a dreadful
thing! They had forgotten the basket of
sandwiches and cakes.

'We left it where we ate our apples,' said Jane
in dismay. 'We must go back. Oh dear, what a
nuisance!'

'It was *your* fault for making me go and see the

stoat's footsteps and follow them,' said Billy.

'It was your fault for being so silly as not to remember the basket!' said Jane. 'Come on. Let's go back.'

But, dear me, they must have taken the wrong path, for though they walked on and on they didn't seem to come to the path they knew.

'I'm so hungry and tired,' said Jane, beginning to cry. 'It must be getting late, Billy. The sun seems quite low.'

On they walked and on, till Jane's legs felt as if they would give way.

'I *must* have a rest,' she said, and she sat down in the crisp snow. Billy sat down too, and looked around him wondering what to do. He was dreadfully hungry, and he longed for the sandwiches that Mummy had made for them.

'Look, Jane!' he said suddenly, and pointed to the bare trees nearby. 'There are some red squirrels. They must have woken up on this lovely day and come to find the nuts they stored away.'

Down to the snowy ground the squirrels leapt, and saw the children. They scampered up to them and made little chattering noises. Then off they went again and began to dig in the snow.

'I do believe they are telling us where their nuts

are!' said Billy, in excitement. 'Come on, Jane. Let's see. I could eat hundreds of nuts, couldn't you?'

The children ran up to the squirrels. One had already uncovered a little store of nuts under the root of an old tree. Another was scraping the snow near a bush, and soon Jane saw a neat little pile of hazelnuts appearing.

The squirrels did not touch the nuts, but let the children take them and crack them. Soon Billy and Jane were having a lovely feast; and didn't they enjoy the nuts! They were so hungry that they thought they had never tasted anything so delicious!

'Oh, thank you, squirrels!' said Jane when she could really eat no more. 'You *are* kind! Now I do wish you could show us the way out of the wood! We're quite lost!'

At once the little red squirrels led the way, looking back for Billy and Jane to follow.

'Well,' said Billy, astonished, 'I wonder if they really *do* know the way! Let's follow them and see.'

They *did* know the way, and in ten minutes the two children were walking home, leaving behind them the little red squirrels, chattering excitedly in the trees.

They found their basket by the roadside, and went home munching cakes. Mummy was so surprised.

'I thought you would have eaten those for your lunch,' she said. Then Billy and Jane told her all that had happened.

'Mummy, do you think it was the same squirrels that feasted on our nuts in the garden?' asked Jane.

'Perhaps,' said Mummy. 'And I expect when they saw you hungry and lost they said, "One good turn deserves another", and came to your help. What a good thing you were kind to them in the autumn!'

Jim and the Princess

JIM was most excited. It was prize-giving day at his school, and although he knew that he had not won any prizes himself it was exciting to think that a real princess was coming to give away the books to the clever boys in the school.

'You boys must be at school at two o'clock this afternoon,' said his teacher. 'Then you will be in plenty of time to prepare for the prize-giving. Jim, you are to present the bouquet of flowers to the Princess. You must practise bowing. Come to me for ten minutes after school this morning, and I will see that you know what to do.'

Jim was full of pride to think that he had been chosen to present the bouquet. How pleased his mother would be! He would be able to see the Princess quite close, too. Oh, he really was very lucky!

He hurried over his dinner, and then put on his very best suit. He washed himself carefully and did his hair. He kissed his mother goodbye, and told her to be sure and be at school by three o'clock to see him give the Princess the flowers.

Then off he went on his bicycle. He had a long way to ride – just over three miles – but he was in plenty of time. He rode off, whistling gaily.

He hadn't gone more than half a mile when a car whizzed by him. At the same moment a terrier dog ran into the road. The car struck it, and sent it spinning into the ditch, yelping with fright.

The car sped on without stopping. Jim leapt off his bike and ran to the dog. It was lying in the ditch, yelping dolefully.

'Poor old chap!' said Jim. 'Let's see what damage has been done. Don't be frightened, old boy. I won't hurt you. I only want to help you. Let me look at your front paws.'

The dog let him do what he wanted. Jim loved dogs, and he was angry to think that the motorist had driven on without stopping to see if he had hurt the dog. He saw that the frightened animal was cut and bruised, and could hardly limp along.

'You haven't a name and address on your collar,' said Jim. 'So I don't know who your master is. Perhaps if I take you along with me a little way we shall meet him, and then he will look after you.'

The dog could not walk, so Jim lifted it up and put it on the saddle of his bicycle. Then he began to wheel the dog along the dusty road.

For half a mile he pushed his bicycle along with the dog, but met no one at all. Then he began to get worried.

'I haven't time to walk all the way to school with you, old boy!' he said to the dog. 'I should be too late for the prize-giving – and I've got to give the bouquet too. Goodness! I'll have to wash myself and dust my coat before then; I'm all dirty again now!'

The dog whined and licked Jim's hand. Jim wondered whatever he ought to do. Should he leave the dog in the ditch again and ride on by himself to the prize-giving?

'No, I simply can't do that!' he thought. 'I won't leave the poor creature alone in the ditch! I'll just have to walk on with him like this, and bathe his paws when I get to school. I'll be late for the prize-giving, and someone else will be chosen to give the bouquet; but I can't help that! I'm not going to leave the dog, even though I shall get into a dreadful row!'

He walked on with the dog, pushing his bicycle along the road. When he had gone two miles he looked at his watch. Ten minutes to three! There was no chance of getting to school in time now!

At that moment a beautiful car came by. It passed him, and then suddenly came to a stop. The lady at the wheel, who was very lovely, called out to him:

'What's the matter with your dog, son?'

'He isn't my dog,' said Jim. 'Someone's car knocked him down, and I found him in a ditch. He couldn't walk, so I'm taking him on my bicycle. The awful thing is that I'm supposed to be at school at three to give a bouquet to the Princess who's coming to our prize-giving!'

'Well, look here, jump into my car and I'll take both you and the dog,' said the lady. 'Put your bicycle into the back.'

'Oh, thank you!' said Jim gladly. 'I'll be there in time for the prize-giving, but I'm afraid I'm much too dirty to be allowed to present the bouquet.'

They sped along the road. In four minutes they were in front of the school gates, and then the most surprising thing happened! All the boys massed in front of the gates began to cheer as if they were mad. They waved their caps and shouted at the tops of their voices.

'Whatever's the noise about?' said Jim in

surprise. 'The Princess isn't here yet, is she?'

'Well, I rather think she is!' said the lady in the car. 'You see, I'm the Princess myself! And you shall certainly give me the bouquet!'

Well, what a surprise that was for Jim! Fancy driving up to the school gates sitting beside the Princess! And, goodness! there was his old bike at the back! And a hurt dog on his knee! Jim went as red as a tomato, and couldn't think what to do or say.

The Princess explained everything to the Headmaster, and he told Jim to take the dog to the school porter to be cared for.

'Then wash yourself and come back quickly,' said the Head, with a twinkle in his eye. 'I'm quite proud of you, Jim!'

When he came back the Princess was standing on the platform, smiling at all the boys. Jim was given the bouquet, and very proudly he presented it with his best bow to the lovely Princess. She took it and thanked him. Then she made a little speech and gave away the prizes.

And, to his very great surprise, Jim got one too! It was a book all about dogs, and in it the Princess had written: 'Special Prize. Presented to Jim Brown for kindness to animals.'

Wasn't he pleased! How everyone clapped!

His mother could hardly sit still in her seat for joy! As for the dog, they couldn't find out who was his owner, so Jim kept him, and a happier couple you really couldn't find!

Old Mother Hubbard

OLD MOTHER HUBBARD lived in a tiny cottage in Pippin Village. She was a thrifty old dame, and only once a year did she really have her cupboard full of nice things – and that was on January the fifth, because that was her birthday, and her dog's birthday too.

Jumpabout, the dog, was a fine fellow. He wasn't very big, but his bark was very loud indeed. He liked his birthday, because Old Mother Hubbard always gave him a large, meaty bone then, besides some chocolate cakes and six sugar biscuits.

'Is our birthday near?' he asked Old Mother Hubbard a hundred times a year – and at last, when Christmas was over, she would say yes, it was coming near. Then Jumpabout would wag his tail and jump about like mad.

The night before their birthday Old Mother Hubbard spoke to Jumpabout, looking very much frightened.

'You must sleep outside the front door

tonight,' she said. 'I have heard that a band of wicked brownies are about, and they steal into people's houses at night and take everything they can. I feel afraid, Jumpabout, so you must sleep on the mat outside the door, then no one will get in.'

Jumpabout said he would; but when the night came he didn't like it a bit. He wasn't afraid of brownies, not he – but it was a freezing cold night, and he didn't like to leave the rug by the warm fire. It was so cosy there, and the mat outside the front door was stiff and hard and cold.

Jumpabout lay there for a little while, and then, when he heard Old Mother Hubbard snoring, he crept into the kitchen again and lay down by the fire. The warmth at once sent him to sleep, and there he lay all night long, snoring just as loudly as Old Mother Hubbard!

He didn't hear the front door pushed open. He didn't see the gleaming eyes of the robber brownies. He didn't hear their footsteps going to the cupboard – he heard and saw nothing but his own dreams.

He awoke early and, hearing Old Mother Hubbard stirring, he ran to the mat outside the door, and lay there looking as if he had spent the whole night long guarding the cottage.

'Oh, poor Jumpabout!' cried Old Mother Hubbard when she saw him. 'You must be cold and hungry! Did you hear anything of the robber brownies?'

'No,' said Jumpabout. 'It's my belief it's just a tale, Mother Hubbard. They didn't come near *here*, anyway, or I should have barked loudly enough, I can tell you.'

'Many happy returns of the day,' said Mother Hubbard, patting him. 'It's our birthday today, you know, and as you have been such a good dog all night long, lying out there in the cold, I shall give you a great, big, meaty bone that I bought from the butcher yesterday.'

She went to the cupboard to get Jumpabout his bone, and the little dog followed her hungrily. But when she got there, oh, dear me! the cupboard was bare – not a thing was in it!

'Why,' gasped Mother Hubbard. 'What has happened? Where's the bone? Where's my birthday cake? Where's the apple pie? Where's the bread? Where are the sugar biscuits and the chocolate cakes I made only yesterday? Oh, you bad dog, you must have eaten them all in the night!'

'I *didn't* take your things!' Jumpabout cried. 'I don't know where they've gone!'

'Well, if you slept out on the mat all night long the brownies couldn't have taken them,' scolded Mother Hubbard. 'So you *must* have eaten them, Jumpabout. I am very much ashamed of you.'

Just then there came a knock at the door, and Mr Tumble, the village policeman, put his head in.

'Are you there, Mother Hubbard?' he asked. 'We've captured the robber brownies, and with them they had a great deal of food. Have you missed any?'

'Oh, yes!' cried Mother Hubbard. 'Bring it in here and let me see it.'

Mr Tumble brought it in and set it on the table. Everything was there except the chocolate cakes, which the brownies had eaten.

'Thank you so much for bringing them back to me,' said Mother Hubbard gratefully. 'Please take these sugar biscuits for yourself, Mr Tumble, in return for your trouble.'

'Thank you very much,' said Mr Tumble. 'And perhaps you'd let me have this bone too, Mother Hubbard, to give to Tips, my dog. It was he who caught the robbers.'

'Of course!' said Mother Hubbard, and she

wrapped the bone up in a bit of paper and gave it to him.

When the policeman had gone Mother Hubbard turned to Jumpabout, who had put himself in the corner.

'*Did* you sleep on the front door mat?' she asked sternly. Then Jumpabout confessed that he hadn't, and said that the brownies must have taken the things when he was fast asleep on the hearth-rug.

'Well, you are a naughty, stupid little dog!' said Mother Hubbard. 'All the things I got for your birthday treat have gone. The brownies ate the chocolate cakes, Mr Tumble has the sugar biscuits, and I have given your bone to his dog Tips. You had better go out to your kennel and think of how naughty you have been.'

Jumpabout went out to his kennel, and he was very miserable all day, and very hungry.

'I deserve to go without anything,' he whined to himself. 'I am a very naughty, horrid little dog, and I've quite spoilt my birthday.'

Mother Hubbard let him stay there till tea-time, then she cut a big piece of her birthday cake and took it out to him.

'You don't deserve it,' she said. 'But if you promise never to disobey again I'll forgive you.'

Jumpabout promised, and gobbled up the birthday cake – and as far as I know he has never been a naughty dog again. Mr Tumble the policeman made up a rhyme about him. Do you know it? It is:

Old Mother Hubbard
Went to the cupboard
To get her poor dog a bone,
But when she got there
The cupboard was bare
And so the poor dog had none!

Jumpabout does *hate* to hear Mr Tumble singing that song!

Enid Blyton

FIFTEEN MINUTE TALES

'Thank you,' said the Queen in a silvery voice. 'What a beautiful umbrella! I do wish I had one like that!'

In this charming collection of tales, the Queen of the fairies borrows Mollie's new umbrella, Niggle the naughty gnome turns over a new leaf, and Mr Prickles the hedgehog drives the horrid red goblins out of Fir Tree Wood. There's also a silly pixie who posts his handkerchief instead of his own party invites and a bad little elf who lands himself in a heap of trouble!

Enid Blyton

TWENTY MINUTE TALES

Suddenly the wooden horse began to gallop down the hill for all he was worth. 'Wherever are we going?' shouted Morris to Alison.

Two children are carried off to Toy-Town – and get the fright of their lives; Harry eats some magic toffee and turns into a hen, and Feefo the pixie dog changes colour! All sorts of strange and surprising things happen in this exciting collection of stories.

Enid Blyton

AMELIA JANE AGAIN

'Amelia Jane, stop!' shouted all the toys in a rage.

Amelia Jane is a very bad doll. She's always making trouble for the other toys in the nursery. She catches them in a butterfly net, she hides their shoes down a mouse-hole, and she pelts them with snowballs. Sometimes the toys play tricks on Amelia Jane too, and then she promises to be good – but it's not long before she's naughty again!

Amelia Jane gets up to more mischief in

Naughty Amelia Jane!
Amelia Jane Gets Into Trouble!
Amelia Jane is Naughty Again!

Enid Blyton

BIMBO AND TOPSY

'Topsy! You are blowing bubbles!' Bimbo cried. 'Oh, you do look funny!'

Bimbo the kitten and Topsy the terrier are the best of friends. They are always playing tricks on one another and getting up to mischief.

They sneak into the larder and gobble up all the food; Bimbo falls down a chimney, and gets his head stuck in a cream jug, and when Topsy is hungry, he eats a cake – of soap! There's no end to their naughtiness!

Enid Blyton

THE ADVENTURES OF THE WISHING-CHAIR

'Oh, Peter, to think we've got a magic chair – a wishing-chair!'

Mollie and Peter have a big secret; in their playroom is a magic Wishing-Chair which can grow wings and take them on flying adventures. They rescue Chinky the pixie from a giant's castle, visit Disappearing Island, and go to a party at Magician Greatheart's castle.

There's more Wishing-Chair magic in *The Wishing-Chair Again*.

Other Enid Blyton titles available from Mammoth

☐	7497 0761 5	**Amelia Jane Again!**	£2.50
☐	7497 0760 7	**Naughty Amelia Jane!**	£2.50
☐	7497 0812 3	**Mr Meddle's Muddles**	£2.50
☐	7497 0813 1	**Mr Meddle's Mischief**	£2.50
☐	7497 0814 X	**Book of Brownies**	£2.50
☐	7497 0815 8	**Book of Fairies**	£2.50
☐	7497 0819 0	**Bimbo and Topsy**	£2.50
☐	7497 0762 3	**Adventures of the Wishing-Chair**	£2.50
☐	7497 0763 1	**The Wishing-Chair Again**	£2.50
☐	7497 0810 7	**The Adventures of Mr Pink-Whistle**	£2.50
☐	7497 0811 5	**Mr Pink-Whistle Interferes**	£2.50
☐	7497 0757 7	**Amelia Jane Gets Into Trouble!**	£2.50
☐	7497 0756 9	**Amelia Jane Is Naughty Again!**	£2.50